Citadel 7 Series

Coming Storm

Thorr's Journey

His gallant actions will spark events affecting the entire Superverse.

His enemies want him dead.

Novella 3

Yuan Jur

Cover art : Ralph Manis/Infinitee Designs

WAADOOM

Australia

Coming Storm by Yuan Jur

ISBN-13: 978-0-9942153-0-7 (Paperback)
ISBN-13: 978-0-9942153-4-5 (E-Book Epub)
ISBN-13: 978-0-9942153-3-8 (E-Book MOBI)

Cover and art design by Ralph Hawke Manis of Infinitee Designs 2017
www.infinitee-designs.com
Book design and production by WaaDoom in association with
Thebookpatch.com
Editing and structure by Charles Wannop and De Chao Peterson

Dedication

To the dedicated Citadel 7 crew. The guys and girls no one hears about. The backers LMA, Editor JDK, Cover art "Ralph the Brush", production manager CW, promotion LA and beta testers NC DW & Co.

You all continue to be awesome. Thanks for helping the Citadel 7 fans Enter The Superverse, a domain created for all wanting to press beyond their comfort zones as their heroes in Citadel 7 stories do, even when the journey may reveal more than they had intended to find.

Orders

"C-date . . . classified.

Location . . . M system restricted Toran Cluster.

Live Timeline, active . . .

Fortress of Bach secure access unfolding thread, stable.

. . . Arrival on the Toran world via Soul Core transfer approved.

Materialization in . . . 3, 2, 1."

CHAPTER

1

A Coming Storm

"Thank you, central. We'll take it from here. Hello Agent. My name is Uniss. I am a Superverse Profiler for the House of Zero—Karmic Evolution Division. We have met before, don't worry, your loss of memory for that previous journey is quite normal. With Central's approval, you have been selected again and assigned to us for this run. My words are presented to you via the universal translator you were chipped with last time. It will translate all languages on your journey into your own common tongue. It is our task, to ensure you arrive as intended with briefing enough to be effective in your role here. For this excursion, you are in the majority an observer. Your decisions and actions by this journey's end could influence far-reaching outcomes for Citadel Council planning that guides all in the Superverse.

"We are here because throughout the Superverse at present there is much trouble festering on this timeline in places it shouldn't. There are other forces at play. We have returned here to Ludd's Heart, a body of land at the center of the Toran planet's Great North Continent. It stands at the epicenter of the growing turmoil. I'll fill you in on what you need to take with you while your four states realign and you acclimatize. Look around us. It is the season of Leaf Fall here, a bitter autumn by your Earth standards. Races on all continents spanning this world have experienced an uncharacteristic rise in violence and mayhem in recent times. Mystics and spiritual leaders of the many races tell stories of a sinister voice on the wind after a dream of warning. They speak of it as godlike. They're almost correct. It's a powerful intelligence alright. We've heard reports of it often masquerading as a benevolent face atop a beautiful sunflower. Each dreamer thereafter would warn the voice on the wind intends great harm to all inhabiting this world. Few paid attention, at first. Those who openly raised alarm in public places would go missing or be found dead in mysterious circumstances. No manner of search ever exposes the culprit. We'll need to tread carefully in this one, Agent. Fear of who might be next has spread like plague. It's burning across Ludd's Heart in whispers, just as the Creeping Death spread between the races a few short years earlier. Only the resilient Scarzen were spared that horror. What is coming this time, though, if it runs its full course, will leave its mark on everyone. Something tells me in time to come, you are mixed up in events here too, Agent. I hope you will help again as you have done in the past.

"Naysayers protesting amongst the Flaxon of Weirawind City in the north, and the Celeron citizens of the West, place suspicion on the gods. It is touted that only they could have such power over so many. Rulers of various domains with grand schemes and machinations of conquest blame the warriors of Scarza. It's because of their little-understood powers of kin and combat prowess. The planet is heading for a total race war, Agent. We can't let that happen. One thing is certain—truth and hearsay are now indistinguishable. Nothing is as it seems.

"Come. We'll transport further southwest now, to the southern frontier." This part of Ludd's Heart is wild, a hard place to survive, Agent. Full of blade grass and skin-burning fire bush. Steep mountainous ridges said to be the spine of a once great beast who made the ground shudder underfoot. It now forms a majestic rugged landscape. All Scarzen clans from the bunker dwellers of Talon East to the outpost inhabitants of High Keeper Jallanaa's Talon South, know this place as the Wilderness of the Beast's Ribs. Its dominance reaches to the west coast of Ludd's Heart where the deep green ocean of Shalane invites seafarers to explore a greater world. Amidst the shoulders of this place are pockets of thick forest that appear like oases of green breaking up the bronze stone terrain. Some of those forests harbor scarzen outpost, communities often many generations old.

We are interested in a resident of one such outpost. His name is Thorr. The outpost's name is Hammer Forge of West Mountain. The scarzen occupying this windy, Stendle-wood forest, aside from their prowess in masonry and armor making, are hardy warriors even by scarzen standards. It is some days before selected young prospects from across Scarza will make their journey to Talon West for assessments. Thorr is one of them. This time is known as their Rite-of-Passage. Now look to your right, to the side of that hill. For this is where the seeds of a far greater story sit with the one we'll find there. Can you see them yet? Legend says; on West Mountain, the harsh winds of Leaf Fall and White Silk sweeping through these woodlands carry the spirit of their ancestors. In particular, one known as Hoxxaa. All scarzen clans know the campfire stories of them from the time they are chest borne. Remember what I speak of here Agent. All know of the voice on the wind who whistles past their dwelling's windows. Hoxxaa, the protector of all scarzen, guards the secret veins of Trilix crystal found in the mountains embracing their bunker strongholds. Scarzen orators say; Hoxxaa himself claims the soul of any non-scarzen suspected of seeking unlawful access inside the mines of Scarza. But he is much much more than that. The southern mine of West Mountain and the Lyran Range to the north are cited as being of special interest to Hoxxaa. Trilix is more than just a curious element unearthed for a kind of salve to mend their bones. It has unique properties specifically affecting scarzen physiology, a rare and mysterious power that protects and invigorates them. Trilix does this in a way that makes them the apex warriors on the Toran world. But even there is a mask for something quite different. The delicate blue shards under scarzen protection come with penalty of death for any unauthorized intruder and their family. The High Keepers of Scarza intend ensuring Trilix never leaves their control. All Scarza is built around that single objective.

In the part of Scarza we now stand called West Mountain, reside some of the most feared of Scarza's front line sentinels. Our target has the potential to be one of them. Demand for such warriors is high amongst Scarza's command elite. There is the one we are interested in, sitting below the brow of that silk grass covered knoll. He likes the quiet there. It overlooks a bend in the Saw Tooth River shaping the landscape at its foot. Thorr has a lot ahead of him. Follow his journey. It's time to leave you now. You'll hear me via your universal translator from time to time. Observe closely, Agent. There is much we must learn for the safety of the entire Superverse.

CHAPTER

2

Sent into Exile

Afternoon sun pressed warm on Thorr's long dreadlocks and the chiseled features of his armor-skin face. In contemplation of his future in weeks to come, he ground a chaw of Kambaa mushroom jerky between his teeth. Happily chewing on the pepper tasting fiber, he took in the surrounding scenery. Sunlight filtered through a dispersing blanket of thin cloud, which made the tree foliage across the slopes look amber at their crest.

I will miss this land, he thought. *Otaa Tralldon says the trees of the north do not have this hue.*

Hunching over he reached for a flower pushing up through the grass from between his feet. He pulled its stem. One of the season's last yellow-orange Dajaa flowers.

Delicate little thing I think I will even miss your kind too. "Maybe it is as Otaa Tralldon says," he told himself as if to someone else. *After what happened, there will be better things to occupy my skill-set at Talon West. Perhaps I can expunge my shame there.* He sighed. *The consult was honorable. The challenge was foisted upon me. I did not welcome it. Had Raldaa withdrawn his remark, I would not have had to pacify him so harshly.*

Thorr looked at the teardrop shaped forearm buckler heavily strapped to his right arm. A mental flash of the last four aggressive strokes delivered by his opponent sped past his mind. They had been meant to do real damage. His eyes fell upon the new score marks on his buckler's upper quarter. They were an indelible reminder of the final strike that had finished their duel and settled the matter. A last fading image of his vanquished clan peer face down in the dirt, head crushed body lifeless fell like a leaf on the floor of his mind.

Perhaps accepting the consequences early is better for all concerned. Otaa is right. This way reprisal is limited. That he has to plead my case is shameful enough, witnesses or not.

The Dajaa flower looked delicate in Thorr's slaa gloved covered fist, a thick fingered wrecking ball many times its size. The feeling of being watched again washed over him. He looked over his shoulder and scanned the hillside down to the water for the threat.

"Don't be a Broz, you're quite alone in this, it's the way it has to be," he muttered.

Instinct told him he'd been followed for several days on his lone walks along the trails, by what or who he couldn't say. No physical threat had ever been discovered when he'd gone to investigate.

"If you keep running around in your head like that, you'll end up like Broznick with brains turned to cornmeal and never see the glory of battle or have a commander's respect."

He twiddled the flower between thumb and finger as his voice of self-worth rattled on inside his head.

"They'll send you off to the Slaa Groves for the rest of your days," he grunted. There they'll have you do nothing more than turn thread for what you've done today, if you don't find your center. There'll be no taking the mantel as Otaa intended now. Otaa is right. Best you accept your fate and become anonymous amongst the ranks of Talon West. There none will know your shame and Hammer Forge will be clear of retribution from High Keeper Jallanaa.

He saw small ribbon fish jump in the slow moving water of the rivers bend. On the other bank, a wild Zukaa bull approached out of the underbrush to the water's edge. He guessed the mature beast looked to weigh in at around the one and a half scarzen ton mark. Its broad muscular chest meant it would be very hard to stop in a charge and it was the season of muster for the swept-back horned wild battering ram. Its shoulders were at least twice the width of Thorr's own and stood seven feet at the shoulder. That meant the beast's heavy muscled head and neck easily matched his ten-foot-tall build eye to eye. Thorr considered the bull carefully for a moment.

At around 375 pounds including armor, he considered at least four good strokes to crack its skull would be needed if he had to. He hoped that didn't become necessary, he had things to think about of higher importance. He watched the Zukaa bull drop its head to drink taking in steady drafts to quench its thirst. Keen eyesight drew his attention to a long shadow under the water approaching on the beast's right. It drifted in closer as if it were a submerged fallen tree trunk pushed by the current, not uncommon for this river. Then he realized, the current was going the other direction. Thorr looked on with keen curiosity. He felt life around him somehow hold its breath in anxious wait to see something play out. As the beast drew in its last drafts of water, the black shadow drew closer. Raising itself to the surface now the life form looked to be ten good scarzen strides long. From what he could see, it was as thick through the body as the length of one of his legs. Steadily, he watched two-thirds of the powerful predator's body flex into a bow. Like a thick piece of Stendle branch under heavy load it made ready to strike. In the next moment, there was a great explosive upsurge in the water right in front of the Zukaa bull's head. Out of the water burst a hideous boney head shaped like a spiny-webbed sinister hand. Snapping over the bulls head with a force that could bend thick iron, the River Jaw Fish claimed its prey. Aggressively, it jerked backward wrenching the bull deeper into the water. A war of wills and self-preservation ensued which made Thorr sit forward with anticipation. Snorting and bellowing, for a moment the bull regained a slight advantage withdrawing toward higher ground. Then the River Jaw asserted its power again, one death roll then another and another. The force of its potent action ripped the Zukaa off its feet, and the animal was pulled mercilessly into the deeper muddy water. Thorr felt at once sadness for the bull's defeat and deeply respectful for the Jaw Fish's power as the victor. There was a last desperate attempt to escape from the bull with some thrashing about breaking the water's surface. Then all signs of struggle stopped and calm returned to the bend in the river as if nothing had happened. Thorr said a small prayer for the Bull's spirit.

The words of Thorr's Otaa, Tralldon, often recited to him from The Scarzen Book of Warrior, rang in his head; Walk with honor as your foundation. *Life is war. Victory or defeat is always determined by one's preparations for it. Honing the skills to realize the aim is key to an honorable death.*

Thorr grunted and nodded to himself then stood. He cast the flower down toward the river's edge. It spun away on the breeze to where the water calmly lapped the shore.

How quickly life can turn hopes in one direction to become new frontiers of another, he thought.

The flower settled to bobble about on the water's edge. The wind and current soon took it away to deeper water like a passenger bound for an unknown destination. Then in a blink, it was gone, snapped up by a fish leaving only a ring of water to mark the moment. A gust of wind blew past from his right. The stark crack of a stick snagged his attention from behind and he looked about with suspicion.

There's that eyes on me feeling again. "Humph . . . nothing." He re-tensioned the strap of his left forearm buckler. *Next, you'll be making enemies of shadows. I'll leave on the morrow.*

Thorr turned and made his way up the trail with strong strides back toward Hammer Forge. He resisted the urge to keep scanning for enemies. He would meet them soon enough.

CHAPTER

3

Walking Alone

A good while passed. Marching back at a stiff pace, Thorr finally topped the hilly rise that offered a south facing view of Hammer Forge in the distance. Amidst a young Stendle wood grove where trunks swayed in a moderate breeze, he saw a familiar face. Boldaa, a Maximum sentinel in armor style and colors of his clan watched his approach. Taller than Thorr by a head, Boldaa held Thorr's personal pet on a tether. Also Hammer Forge's mascot, the prehistoric-looking reptile had orange scales and spiked head that reached to Boldaa's upper thigh. The lizard's heavy spiked collar had the name Borzzaackeem, which translates in other simpler tongues as, *Dave*, branded into the leather. Nostril to tail-tip Dave measured two standard scarzen strides long.

Thorr's older offspring carried a well-stuffed travel satchel in the other hand. Boldaa outweighed his younger brother by several standard stones. He was more muscular in build too, if that was possible. He carried on his back a heavy haft battle-mattock. It had a snub nose for crushing bone on one end and cruel talon on the other.

"Are you going somewhere?" asked Thorr.

"No," said Boldaa clipping the word. "You are."

Thorr frowned. "I had intended to leave on the morrow."

"No, you're leaving now. The unit patrol leader, Morlaak is insisting you accompany them back to Talon South. They intend you stand trial for your unreasonable response in the umm . . . friendly consult."

"What!" blasted Thorr. "No quarter was given me for respectful withdrawal and before I ended it, that Broz attempted an insult subjugation. It would have humiliated our entire outpost."

"Now find your center little brother," pushed Boldaa. "You've done no true wrong, technically. You have our Otaa's support who approves of your actions under the circumstance. Under normal protocols, the tables of fault could not be turned. But the one you so unexpectedly left in the dirt this morning had name of influence in Talon South, big influence."

"What do you mean?"

"That Talon South unit leader, Morlaak. The one who stood back as the challenge unfolded."

"Yes, what about him?"

"Well, he's not about to wear the blame for an incident involving a subordinate who has ties to our High Keeper."

"He is the unit commander. It *is* his responsibility. Why did he not put an end to the nonsense before it got out of hand? He made no attempt to stop the illegal challenge."

"Politics I suspect. He wouldn't undermine the public actions of the nephew of High Keeper Jallanaa."

Thorr's expression suddenly turned to one of aghast realizing the weight of the situation.

"That's right, you unceremoniously planted Solaak Trazaan, High Keepers favorite cousin."

Thorr sighed thinking on what was unfolding.

"Shak, they set me up," said Thorr clenching a fist in frustration.

"Appears so," nodded Boldaa. "According to Otaa, the privileged broz Solaak was on his first commissioned patrol. Tralldon said it looks like they'd taken Solaak along to get his muzzle wet in the field. The ignorant Broz ignored your lack of rite-of-passage band on your braids. At first, before the unexpected outcome, the others probably thought the joke was on Solaak for his misreading of the situation. Solaak mistook your size for age. A common mistake amongst the bunker bourns meeting our wilderness cousins for the first time. To them, we *all* look the same, more mature in years. Boldaa winked at his sibling. He wanted to make a statement. Like I said, the joke was on him."

Thorr shook his head. "That Broz chose to take exception to a passing comment directed entirely at someone else. Then spat at our Otaa's name when I rebutted his foolish slander. He stepped forward and demanded satisfaction. I addressed the matter as was my rite according to The Book of Warrior, passage twenty-one. I gave him space to withdraw."

"You did," agreed Boldaa.

"He refused and pressed for satisfaction. So I gave him what he demanded so boldly."

Thorr looked down and placed a hand on Dave's head, who nuzzled his keeper back.

"Pride saw him find his way to the halls of our Ancestors," said Boldaa.

"That's right. I didn't even claim his weapon as is my right."

Thorr stubbed the toe of his boot into the ground in frustration.

"That kind of made it worse," said Boldaa with a bit of a wince. "You should have at least picked it up and handed it to Morlaak, instead of kicking it to one side like trash and storming off. It was an embarrassment to the fallen one's name and his unit."

"He wore battlefield commission braids," said Thorr. "I treated him accordingly."

"That you did little brother, that you did. The ancestors will stand with us all in this, I'm sure. There is however, a last cruel ligature in this and it has you around the neck."

Thorr looked at his brother.

"I am an untried pup, what more can go wrong?"

"Not after today," said Boldaa nodding with satisfaction.

"What do you mean?"

"You kicked the shak out of that Broz right and proper in front of his commander. Proud of you. But, Solaak's commander is holding you responsible for instigating the situation causing the demise of one of privilege. He will report it that way to Keeper Malforce, personally."

"So now they want a head to cover up their mess," said Thorr.

"Someone has to pay. By Morlaak's demeanor when he left, it won't be him if I'm any judge."

Thorr looked at his brother gobsmacked.

Boldaa shrugged. "Aww, you were not to know. I thought your tactics to undo him showed real sparks of a front line sentinel. Personally, I would have dislocated his pelvis first."

"You always were more subtle than I brother, not," said Thorr. "So now what?"

"Otaa Tralldon sent this." Boldaa handed Thorr the shoulder pack. "Otaa has gone on record demanding his right as outpost clan head to bear the burden of the consultation. He orders *you* to go and earn back our clan's favor.

"How?" asked Thorr.

"By bringing glory to our name after you have passed your rite-of-passage at Talon West. Tralldon has petitioned the Master at Arms, Dorjaa, by Sellenor messenger. Dorjaa will help you. Once the handover is sealed you become the property of the academy and can't be touched till you are released for duty. By that time we hope to have the mess sorted.

"I see," said Thorr.

"By air, the Sellenor will reach Talon West Bunker at final gate call tonight. Tralldon's petition aims to have you sanctioned for Special Forces."

"Special Forces, stugat! He does have high expectations. Told me my clever head would be best used for breaking rock day before yesterday."

Boldaa's expression shifted to a gentler place and an expression of brotherly endearment emerged.

"You underestimate yourself. In his eyes, little brother. You are the best of us, as such, he'll not see your potential lost in an untidy mess such as this. He wants more to come of your existence than just filling your head with song lines, and having the power to take down a zukaa bull with one blow from your buckler. He believes you have the ability to raise our worth in the eyes of high command.

"No pressure."

"None at all brother. Otaa said Dorjaa, who is a warrior of considerable influence in Talon west, owes him a favor. Don't let Otaa down. Your identity scroll is in the pack. Now say goodbye to Dave and become a shadow not to be tracked, before Morlaak rounds you up and things turn ugly."

Thorr knelt down and placed a heavy gloved hand on the animal's head. Dave made a gurgling sound and snorted nuzzling into Thorr's chest nearly toppling him.

"Woo there, little warrior," said Thorr warmly. "It's alright, I'll be back. You stay with Boldaa. He'll look after you. You can't come where I'm going this time. I will send for you when this is done and my new posting is set."

Thorr stood and extended a hand to his brother who met him with an accepting forearm grip of respect.

"Tell Otaa I will return honor to Hammer Forge," said Thorr.

"You better or I'll knock your head with my mattock not too gentle. You have three days to make the journey."

Thorr saluted, a sign of respect for his brother by bowing slightly and passively presenting the right side of his face, eyes down. He turned and with the afternoon waning, headed north-east for the Great North Road.

✷

Thorr marched with determined steps for some hours after leaving Boldaa and Dave. Soon shadows of coming night grew long at the foot of tree and stone. The late hour urged Thorr to consider setting his night camp. He had a place in mind, knowing the terrain and its dangers. Stepping along a ridge that overlooked the Great North Road away in the distance, Thorr noticed heavy cloud gray cloud forming above.

"Hmm, could be rain," he told himself.

He moved across a ridge littered with Stendle trees. The ground was plagued with biting insects. Masses of small night clicker wings infested the thick clump grasses he moved through. At the top of the rising slope, some strides past being free of the annoyances, he found the small grove of trees he was looking for.

"There will allow the warmth of a concealed fire," he told himself.

He moved inside the grove to clear himself space at the foot of a bronze stone overhang. Pulling his general duties knife from the sheath at the back of his utility belt, Thorr cut some bracken for a mattress. He then used a natural stone depression on the ground to build his evening fire. Gathering fallen wood, twigs and moss, he made a small pyramid and struck his flint stones at the base to ignite the moss. After a couple of attempts, a small yellow-green flame spread from the moss to timbers. It made the space feel instantly more appealing. In no time, the flames of a near smokeless fire glimmered away. Inside his pack, he found some slaa-cloth wrapping containing some smoked-dried Jaw Fish and corn biscuits. Munching on a biscuit, he added some water from a small skin in the pack to a kidney shaped bowl taken from the pack's side pocket. He placed the vessel in the hot ashes at the side of the fire and waited for it to boil. Above, the tree tops rustled in a thin breeze and early stars signaled the arrival of night. The water surface in the vessel soon began to turn on the boil. Thorr added a piece of Jaw Fish and wild salt bush to season the broth. The aroma pleased him and soon he began his supper.

After dunking the last of the corn biscuit in the broth, Thorr finished his soup thinking on recent events. At his feet, a Nutt-back beetle waddled past the sole of his boot heading straight toward the fire.

"That will ruin your evening little Drommal," he told the insect as if it understood.

Thorr reached down to point a swirling finger at the insect. Using his kin ability, a form of kinetic will projection innate to all scarzen, Thorr rolled the beetle away from a certain death. He flicked it off into the bushes nearby.

"There you go. Make a good name for your clan."

He turned his attention to repacking his kit for an early start and long journey on the morrow. Done to his satisfaction, Thorr lay down to begin his evening ritual of memorizing the stars. As always, flat on his back using a steady meditative breathing stroke while counting the far away bright specks, Thorr put himself to sleep in no time.

Hours passed; the embers of the fire died to a low smolder and full night blanketed the forested ridge to the sound of night birds and Crick beetles. Scarzen are known to be light sleepers. When a last hot ember from the fire ashes popped the sound prompted Thorr to crack an eye open. At first, he remained ready to drift back off to sleep, but then as though a gentle hand touched him on the shoulder he became aware of another living presence directly opposite. The moonlight provided an outline of an individual in a gray long coat and hat sitting on a low flat stone on the other side of the fireplace.

Realizing the individual was no scarzen, Thorr feigned a *sleeping giant* deciding what to do next. He reached out with all his senses to feel if any others were on his flank. Then he noticed to the individual's left, the outline of a small stocky canine sitting next to him. The dog's small size and lack of chest armor suggested it wasn't used for consults.

"Easy now big fella," said the intruder, no threat in his tone. "We both know you're well awake." They noted the slightest shift in the shoulder tension of the scarzen. "We are not here to consult. We just want to talk."

In the time it would take to clap hands twice, Thorr had rolled to his feet and activated the impaler on his right buckler by making a fist. He stood to his full imposing nine feet tall. Arm drawn full rearward ready to rain heavy damage onto the invaders, Thorr saw neither canine nor seated master move in fear or aggression.

"State your race and your intentions Broz," Thorr ordered using Ludd common tongue. "Or prepare to lose that body and stand before your ancestors."

The camp intruder remained seated eyes fixed on Thorr. His fingers threaded together on his lap, he gave the impression of being totally un-phased by the order.

"We concede your dominance of this space warrior," said the Traveler. "My name is Uniss, we mean you no harm. We," he pointed to his scruffy canine companion   "are not Flaxon or Chou. Nor of Celeron clan for that matter. Our lands are far from any of your borders. We number only two. You would honor us if you would share a fire and exchange of words before the sun rises. We have need of your aid and perhaps something useful for you in return."

Thorr pulled his head back with a twisted expression as if pinched on the nose. What caused him to relax his aggressive posture was that the traveler, Uniss, spoke to Thorr in his own West Mountain dialect, perfectly. Thorr squeezed his fist and the buckler's 18-inch long impaling spike retracted. Thorr eyed the dog with curiosity. She stood as though on cue and wagged her tail.

"Please, this won't take long," said Uniss gesturing for the scarzen to sit.

Curiosity dominated his thoughts now. Thorr complied and took a position at the fireplace opposite. Picking up a few sticks he tossed some into the ashes and stirred the fire with another to rekindle the flames.

"Where did you learn our tongue to speak it so with such candor. Even the Celeron merchants who daily walk our trading trails do not have such talent."

"I am a close friend of the Keeper of the Brasheer," said Uniss.

The mere mention of the title Brasheer from an outsider had Thorr's interest peeked. He leaned forward a hand on one knee pressing Uniss with a glare of keen interest. With elevated respect for the traveler's intimate knowledge of scarzen hierarchy and secret culture, a plethora of questions came to mind.

"You have spoken to the witch of the mountain?" asked Thorr.

"Well, I wouldn't call her a witch, your Mistress Farron might take exception there, and it's ill advised to be on the side of her contempt. Yes, we have had many dealings over the years. We help each other out from time to time."

"Humph," Thorr grunted. "Would that I could be in her employ and train under her guidance I would gladly lay down my life."

"Careful what you wish for tall and muscular. Your paths may yet have a chance to cross."

"Not with the shame I now carry," said Thorr in lament. "No officer of the Brasheer would apprentice me now with what I've done. I will be glad if I am permitted to earn my rite-of-passage and serve Scarza on the front line. Though I expect to be arrested the moment I report in at the Talon West Gate."

Thorr dropped his head in shame.

"Well . . . not everything is as it seems my friend. I'll bet the ancestors have a surprising path planned for you. Remember your scarzen book of warrior directive seven; *though your enemy's standing appears superior before the coming of battle, victory is never determined by reputation. Ignore the bard's tales, examine what is in front of you and the ground he chooses to duel upon, your victory can be found there.*"

Thorr nodded. "I am still considering my Otaa's first directive."

"What is that?" asked Uniss.

"Don't suck at being a warrior. Life will be dishonorably short."

Thorr looked up to his new associate who smiled and coughed a short laugh at the remark.

"I think you must be as noble and hardy as they come. Now hear what I have to say and I'm sure the ancestors will hold you in good favor."

"What do you wish to share?" asked Thorr.

"Tomorrow, when you descend the other side of this ridge to the Great North Road, there is high probability you will encounter a merchant wagon train. They will be heading west to Bon city. As a scarzen warrior of West Mountain encountering an outland convoy in you outpost's jurisdiction, you have a duty to ask their business. Particularly if unaccompanied by a scarzen patrol, and this one won't be. Check the driver's authority to transport goods through Scarza. They're carrying… merchandise that will be of interest to your superiors in Talon West."

"I am only versed in common Chicaa," said Thorr. "My skill in the high written language is minimal. How would I know if there *is* contraband being hauled if I don't recognize any inconsistency in the manifest?"

"Oh, I think it will be pretty obvious… if you look closely. You won't have to worry about the official-looking papers after that. You might like to take a special interest in the wagons with a deeper belly." Uniss stood. "Report your findings to the head of security at Talon West."

"Where are *you* going then?" asked Thorr.

"We have some things to do in league with what we have just spoken of. We can't be seen together. Should anything come to mind after we depart, you would be ill-advised to mention it."

Uniss stepped forward and extended a hand. "We appreciate your help," said Uniss.

Thorr accepted Uniss's hand closing his own huge grip around Uniss's own. The moment that occurred a bubble of space-time around Thorr froze.

"Sorry my large friend, but you are going to have to do this without memory of us. Follow the directives I've given you. Nod in agreement." Thorr nodded. "Good. I've no doubt we'll meet again for the first time in near future. Naught's grace protect you scarzen." Uniss looked to his canine companion.

"Do you still think he has real potential to affect the outcome of what we are dealing with?" she asked.

"I do," said Uniss looking back at Thorr.

"His file on future life potential had several possibilities not necessarily in keeping with our objective, though," said Dog, "And Herrex' influence saturates this world now and in particular the scarzen."

"A Scarzen's will is very robust against manipulation of the mind," said Uniss. "And this one is stronger in will than many of his race. I have a good feeling about this one. He is definitely part of the greater puzzle somehow." Uniss looked about as if other eyes might be watching. "Come on Dogg. The wind is shifting, know what I mean. Time to see if we can locate and sort some of the bigger problems out."

"Let's do it," said Dogg in her educated Earth world English accent.

Uniss let go Thorr's hand. Then both he and Dogg stepped back. The base of their feet began to glow and two silver shafts of light thrust up from under them punching skyward. The energy field dissolved the two from the space leaving only a residual sound of electrostatic to mark their departure. Then that too faded into a vacuous quiet. Seconds later, Thorr lurched forward as if something that had held him up suddenly let go. He caught himself feeling mildly concussed and shook his head. Looking around he scanned for any sign of intrusion.

"What in the name of the ancestors just happened?" he asked himself.

Placing the heel of one hand to his head as though he had drunk something far too cold, the fogginess in his mind cleared. In the next moment, he felt as though he'd stepped beyond some vail back to consciousness. All his normal senses and coordination returned.

He looked to the stars wanting to gauge the time and then tried to remember how his evening had played out, but could not. Scratching his head, Thorr gathered his kit and kicked the fire over with dirt. It was time to make his way down the ridge for the Great North Road.

CHAPTER

4

The Intercept

The opening morning offered a crisp breeze from the west and a cloudless surreal aqua sky. Though quite beautiful, Thorr knew such a sky announced the turn of bad weather coming.

The way down the north ridge was steep in places, easy to slip if steps were not taken with care. Everywhere the forest floor was littered with bushels of red fallen leaves with the colder cycle in play. They often obscured the many hidden dangers existing away from the safety of the roads and trails. It was well known the wilderness alone in Ludd's Heart could be very treacherous, even without any villainous opportunists or predators that roamed the wooded terrain. He recognized and avoided several Grey Shale pockets. The innocuous looking patches of loose gray stone slivers could trap and swallow a careless scarzen instantly up to his neck. If that occurred, in a matter of minutes no trace of their presence would be seen, aside from their last footprints at the edge of the death trap. Halfway down the ridge, Thorr passed a thicket of low standing Fire Bush saplings. The stunted gnarled tree's orange and black speckled leaves bore a yellow slick.

Best avoid that, he thought.

He knew well they formed the basis of a favorite poison used by Quall Assassins'. It could, if skin made contact, send the recipient into hallucinogenic delirium in several hours. Thorr avoided it by following a well-used wildlife trail offering safer places to tread. Following the Bug Eye goat trail into an ever-thickening forest of Knott Trees, the way down often traversed the steep descent by snaking its way along the ridge. Often it would turn back on itself to the lower level to continue. Near the bottom, Thorr passed a carcass of a large Tunnel Snoot. Partly devoured, it had been put to death by something sizable. Something hungry enough to get past the Snoot's jaws and rippling hide body armor to expose the omnivore's soft underbelly. Blackberry Bum flies had already moved in to begin nature's clean up. Below the tree line in the distance, the terrain leveled out with a gentle incline running from East to West. There the planes grasses took over as the dormant flora in this natural corridor.

Running parallel near the foot of the ridge, Thorr could now see an intersecting road that also ran east-west. He knew by its position that only a mile or so further this road would meet the junction of The Great North Road, which would take him on to Talon West Bunker. To his left, the road disappeared around a natural shoulder of the steeper ground.

Suddenly in the mid-distance, he heard the sound of a stockwhip crack, and then the graveled call of a Wagon Master urging his horses on. Thorr focused his will and applied his blur skill which saturated all surfaces in direct contact with him. The action caused his body, armor and buckler surfaces to shimmer and mimic the hue of his surroundings so as to obscure his form. To any who had not seen the action occur, even standing right next to him they would be totally ignorant of his presence. He could see several wagons with clear Celeron markings that would alert any scarzen patrol to their alliance with Scarza. Half of the wagons were covered in a high hoop of calico, obscuring their inner cargo. Two of the wagons were flat covered and looked deeper in the beds than the others.

They seemed to be carrying a mix of boxes, or maybe barrels and crates with who knows what inside, thought Thorr.

Each wagon had a driver and two escorts, one seated next to the driver and one standing on a sentry step on the right side of the wagon behind the front wheel. Only the sentry appeared armed with a sheathed long blade. Thorr noted a long shafted pike standing mounted vertically behind him in arms reach.

Humph, he thought, *so little defense for so much cargo. Why do outland traders traveling unescorted through here from the jungles in the east have such unconcern for their safety? They're either stupid or have a concealed defense inside those wagons.*

Some deeper urge rose for Thorr to intercept them. As they drew closer the third wagon hit a deep pothole in the road that jarred it's axel. When the shakeup occurred, Thorr's keen hearing picked up several voices crying out in discomfort. He frowned.

"That did not sound like livestock. Hmm." *And there's nothing to say that the wagon is carrying any. I am duty bound to enquire as to the reason for any travelers' strange behavior in these territories.*

His conscience compelled him to fulfill that obligation, but instead he hesitated, arguing with himself.

The less who see my movements until I am at Talon West the better, he thought.

As the wagons rumbled past, again from the first flatbed wagon came cries of pain when it hit another sharp-edged hole in the road. The driver turned and shouted to the back of the wagon in common tongue speaking to whoever or whatever made the ruckus to be quiet. Now the urge to investigate kicked his sense of duty over the line.

They are hiding something Hmmm. *Live contraband cannot be allowed to pass. I would truly be branded a rogue if I failed my Otaa again in this duty.* Let us see what they are concealing.

Decision made, Thorr turned and with all the speed his legs could muster, he broke left and headed for the other side of the bluff to intercept the wagons.

CHAPTER

5

Twisted Destinies

As individuals, scarzen are cunning, formidable warriors. Their combat ability on most any ground makes them impressive to watch in the full chaos of battle. There are few who can put them down and live to fight another campaign. When they fight en-masse an enemy does well to avoid their frontline battle circles at all cost.

Even over the disagreeable ground, Thorr's steps set down as sure in full sprint as when he might choose to stroll on the open flat. Racing for the bluff in the short distance to catch them by surprise, he zig-zagged through the trees. Making little sound, even though his size would suggest such pace and silent steps were impossible, he reached the bluff well ahead of the wagons. His position overlooked the bend on the blind side to the road below. Without breaking stride, Thorr leaped off the edge of the bluff to drop some 20 feet to the road below. He hit the ground with a small *thud* and finished in a crouch. A plume of powdered dust billowed up from his boot soles as he stood. In the moment of silence, off to his left his attention was drawn hearing a faint whisper carried on the breeze. It sounded like a villainous cackle at first of someone old. Then followed the hushed warning of . . . *jeopardy*. When he could see no one to own the words the warning unsettled him for a moment.

Then Thorr swung his attention to face his approaching quarry. Rolling up the gentle slope approaching the bluff the sound of a cracking whip and whistles from the driver announced their turning of the bend. Soon, the leading team of heavy shouldered black horses hauling the first long wagon came plodding into view, snorting and harnesses jangling as they pulled their load along. Still obscured from clear view by his blur skill, Thorr waited for the first and part of the second horse teams to appear. Dead center of the wagon train's path he readied himself spacing his feet for action. Then he made himself plain to see. His formidable size and surprise caught the view of the leading team driver immediately. Thorr held his position presenting an impassable obstruction. Seeing the scarzen sentinel, the Wagon Master straightened in surprise and pulled on the reins to halt his transport. He reached to haul on the wheel brake shouting *"WOO Charger, WOO there!"* to his team.

The wagon groaned to a halt as the driver stamped on the wheel brake to stop his wagon rolling backward. A guard standing on a foot pedestal at the side of the wagon stepped down. He unhooked a pike and with some courage stepped forward several paces ready to do his duty. Thorr considered the small threat for barely a moment.

"You are either stupid or ready to meet your ancestors," he told the guard. "Keep your weapon checked, I am not here to spread your entrails on my bread, I am only here to fulfill a duty to my Otaa."

He focused back on the male glaring at him from the driver's seat. Stocky built for a Celeron male in typical well-traveled trail clothes and duster, he certainly looked the part. The hard faced Wagon Master, wore a battered hat above bushy untidy eyebrows, beady eyes, and a thick mustache. He challenged Thorr in a hoarse tone.

"In the name of thunder scarzen, haven't we parlayed enough this round? What do you want!

Thorr said nothing at first considering what the Celeron had just said.

Hmmm . . . No word was mentioned of such a caravan passing through at night's news in recent times. That is strange, he thought. *And why are they using this hard backroad? There are easier paths for wagons such as these.*

"There was no announcements of trade wagons passing through this way by scout or patrol in last days. From where do you hail?" Thorr asked the Wagon Master aloud.

"We are on an urgent errand by order of King Karnor. Stopping this transport will see you disciplined most harshly. Step aside or answer to a higher authority for your misjudgment."

Thorr considered the Celeron's manner and body language for a moment.

He looks unnecessarily agitated, Thorr thought.

"Why so nervous Wagon Master?"

"Having one of you sky-tall blade wielders jump out in front would scare the britches off anyone in these parts." The Wagon Master looked around. "Wait a minute. Where's the rest of your patrol? You look more like you're on a journey than walking patrol."

Thorr gripped subtly the strap of his shoulder pack feeling a hint of his ruse beginning to unravel. There's no way back now, must play on, he thought.

"I am the forward scout. I may have need to detain you, Celeron, till my unit commander arrives if *you* refuse to cooperate. He is not so understanding as I."

"What! Who do you think you are! Get out of the way bone head. We are on King's business!"

The Wagon Master went to urge the horses forward and Thorr grabbed the bridle on the neck of the closest animal with a determined grip. Thorr held the horse team fast with little effort.

"You are passing through the dominion of Hammer Forge," Thorr said sternly. "By order of clan leader Tralldon who enforces the common law of this Scarzen jurisdiction, all outland caravans *will* submit freely to inspection, or have the caravan leader detained for prosecution. Refuse, and I will be forced to consult. I offer this request for the last time. Will you present your passage documents and yield to the small inconvenience of routine search? Or must I enforce the law?"

An armed guard stepped forward in a show of defiance. Thorr looked to him casually and clenched his left fist activating the buckler's impaler.

"Careful little Celeron. I won't think twice about sliding you on that toothpick butt to crown."

The Celeron halted his advance. A momentary awkward silence fell on all in eyeshot. The nerve of the pikeman finally gave way after a snarled shift in Thorr's expression bid him press the point no longer. The guard looked to the Wagon Master for direction. With a swing of his head, the Wagon Master ordered the guard to stand down.

"Hey! What's the holdup?" called the driver of the second wagon.

The first Wagon Master shot a look over his shoulder. "Shut your hole back there."

Thorr watched the gruff individual turn and snap a gaze of discontent back on him.

"Alright . . . thunderin' horse shak. Make your inspection then," barked the Wagon Master as if he was in charge. "Put those pig stickers away and do your duty. Just be quick about it."

Thorr retracted both buckler impalers and approached the Wagon Master. Standing alongside him, though the Wagon Master's sitting position was lofty, Thorr still looked slightly down upon him as he held out a hand.

"Travel passage," he said monotone.

Regardless of Thorr's intimidating presence, the Wagon Master kept his cantankerous disposition, grumbling as he took a crimson leather cylinder from behind his seat. It had the Celeron royal seal of two crossed Holly leaves over a large antlered deer. The Wagon Master uncapped the cylinder and extracted a gold bordered scroll. With a snide expression, he thrust it toward the scarzen.

"You better be sure you know what you're doin', Leather Back. Don't say I didn't warn ya."

Thorr took and unrolled the document doing his best to look like he knew what to look for reading carefully. He kept a straight face understanding little of what the scroll truly meant. All he could deduce on seeing the sophisticated script from the Celeron High Court were a few inserted scarzen words. Words such as the one for the Celeron peoples of Bon City, which was, Nooktaa, meaning, Seafarer. He did, however, have a raised eyebrow at the wax-pressed seal of High Keeper Jallanaa of Talon South at the bottom right.

"Does that thick head of yours even know what it's readin', hmmm . . . satisfied yet?" grumbled the Wagon Master.

Thorr looked at him squarely. "You are a long way from your boats, Nooktaa."

In the short distance, Thorr suddenly heard as the others did, a muffled cry. He noted the Wagon Master, had the smallest flicker of concern in his eyes.

"I'm headin' just as my course intends," said The Wagon Master trying to keep Thorr's attention.

Thorr rerolled the scroll and handed it back glaring straight at the Wagon Master. He let the moment hang enough to make the Celeron need to shift in discomfort.

"I'll only detain you a moment longer. Keep your rollers locked. Do not move forward until I return," ordered Thorr.

Turning to the back of the wagon he stepped off to inspect the cargo. The first two wagons seemed to have nothing out of order. Thorr noticed all the Celeron crews of these transports deliberately avoiding eye contact, not uncommon in Celeron custom to show indifference. Nothing took his interest until he stopped alongside the third wagon which stood fully out of eye shot from the leading wagon crew. His standing height gave him good view across the cargo and he remembered this was the wagon that had caught his interest from the ridge. It and the last wagon were built very differently from the others. Both had a much deeper belly suggesting another reason for use.

Unless . . . there is space in-between, he thought.

Thorr put his shoulder bag down by the rear wheel to investigate further to the increasing concern of the Wagon Master who Thorr knew was watching him closely. He looked for a side latch or panel for underbelly storage and saw none. He checked the other side and back. They were the same. He could feel the others watching getting restless.

What are you hiding?

He knew there must be something to be found and glanced at the driver who kept his eyes forcibly straight forward unlike the others at a distance. Then he noticed that the pinched-faced guard on the other side of the wagon had drawn his dagger.

The guard dropped his eyes and seemed to be looking down at something, gently wiping his blade against the side boards of the wagon. Thorr glared at the guard, still inspecting the wagon with a feeling hand. He spoke to the guard soft but with intent.

"I ate three of those toothpicks and the hands of the ones who offered consult for breakfast." Thorr outstretched a hand fingers splayed and projected a repel field of kin to knock the guard off his perch. The force slammed him against the bank arms spread wind knocked out keeping him pinned.

"Don't," said Thorr.

The guard swallowed and gasped trying to suck in a breath of air.

"Okay," wheezed the guard.

Thorr released the pressure of his kin field and the guard's body slumped and his arms fell limp. He slowly sheathed his blade eyes down passively. Thorr went back to his inspection. Leaning against the wagon he reached to grab and throw off a corner of an oiled muslin cover to inspect the cargo. With his action came a second *bump* and a whimpering cry from somewhere underneath.

Leaning back to look at the side of the wagon, between the cracks and a large knothole, he saw wide frightened eyes staring back at him. Surprised, he stepped back toward the front of the wagon. Then he sensed a threat closing in. He rolled a quick look up to the driver who he saw pulling a long knife from a hidden panel behind his legs. Then, from behind to his right, he caught sight of another guard holding his pike at the ready attempting a stealthy approach intending an ambush. The Wagon Master suddenly lashed out with a yell, which distracted Thorr. Yelling with aggression, he struck wildly with his blade at Thorr's neck.

Thorr easily met the stroke having a far longer reach and blocked it with his buckler. Swiftly he activated the impaler of his other buckler and punched it through and upward into his assailant's torso.

"Bad gamble!" Thorr said lifting his skewered enemy with one arm like a side of roast on a spit.

Thorr flung the dead body at the other pikeman attempting a thrust at his femoral artery. The collision of the airborne driver's body and the pike-wielding guard knocked him head over tail. His weapon spun upward from his lifeless grip. Thorr caught the blade with a casual outstretched hand. Dexterously, he flipped the weapon. Shaft vertical with eighteen inches of spearhead ominously pointing down, he took two strides and drove the pike's business end in. The action forced the pike through the Celeron's body finishing two feet into the hard ground underneath. The driver of the last wagon let out a shrill whistle an alert to call all allies to help.

"Take vengeance lads, there's only one of 'em!" he bellowed.

In moments Thorr caught sight of all the other crews heading his way weapons ready.

Internally Thorr's mood held steady.

"So it's a consult you're asking for," he said to all approaching. "Happy to oblige."

Assailants approached him from two sides unleashing their best killing strokes. One Celeron climbed to the driver's seat of the nearby wagon. War axe raised overhead, he heroically dove at his scarzen enemy intending to deliver a lethal blow. Thorr met the determined aggressor in the chest with a brutal thrust of his impaler and swung the dead body aside like discarded refuse. The dead Celeron's released axe flew through the air. It lodged in the stomach of one individual considering retreat cutting him down in grizzled cries of agony. Horse teams began to panic amidst the violence wanting to flee. The wagon near Thorr began to wheel around out of control. Hitting a hump of earth it lifted about to roll on top of him. Thorr kicked into the wagon's side boards with a heavy boot and set the wagon back on all four wheels. The counterforce of his action caused the lynchpin for the main team's traces to dislodge. The horses broke free trampling another assailant and galloped off. With the broken side boards of the wagon falling away and some panicked jostling about from inside, the inner contents of six bound females spilled to the ground. Thorr recognized their race immediately by their body coverings as Minima. The warrior women from the southern reaches of Ludd's Heart and the only true close allies to the scarzen.

"A slave caravan," he groaned in disgust.

The sight of them in unlawful bondage turned his anger to rage. He applied his blur skill intending all experience an uncompromising grizzly end. Almost invisible to his enemies now, with chilling surgical precision, Thorr methodically hunted down each enemy and dispatching them with crushing blows from his buckler or a ruthless bone-shattering kick to neck or pelvis. One enemy after another was destroyed and cast aside.

Only one opponent, the first Wagon Master, had the good sense to flee before it was too late, or so he thought. Thorr saw him sprinting away legs racing in a panic from the killing field. He was carrying something bright and awkward under one arm. Passing a stunted dead tree, the Celeron chanced a look over one shoulder to see if he was being hunted. His view was immediately blocked by a speeding stone half the size of his head, hurled by Thorr. A clap of hands later, and the primitive projectile crushed his skull. The stone's kinetic impact was so strong it flipped the body legs over head to be lost from view amongst the dirt and blade grass.

Seeing the bolting Celeron fall, Thorr wasted no time in turning to the prisoners who he'd seen spill from the wagon's concealed compartment.

All four girls sprawled on the ground were tied and shackled. One was holding her arm in considerable pain. Another struggled to get free, looking at Thorr with wild terrified eyes for what he might do to them too. He moved swiftly to the nearest girl who was threshing about. She squealed and tried to kick at him as he knelt down beside her. Thorr brushed her feeble effort aside and she fell to one side.

"Stop your nonsense I'm here to help," said Thorr.

The female raised up on her elbows. She wore a shoulder to ankle servant's dress and moccasins. Around the girl's neck, he spotted a gold locket on a fine chain. It was a well-crafted piece.

Hmm, that would definitely be beyond the weight of a servant girl's purse, he thought.

"Borseem, borseem," Thorr said softly holding out a placating hand.

She looked at him terrified clearly ignorant of his meaning. He then remembered to speak in common tongue.

"You are in no danger from me young maiden. I am going to help you. We must speak quickly. I will ask, you will respond. Nod if you agree." The girl nodded with caution in her eyes. "I'm going to take your mouth impairment off."

Thorr reached behind her head. Using his thick, but dexterous fingers Thorr removed the gag. The girl shook her head and spat the dirt and grit from her mouth.

"I do not know how much time we have," said Thorr. "Who are you? Where does your clan reside?"

"Untie me now War Terror, or you shall suffer the same wrath as those who have dared take a Minima citizen for the slave trade."

"War Terror. That is a term used only by the Minima warrior class for scarzen clan allies. Then you are from the jungles of the west?"

"No," said the girl. "We both know the Minima stronghold is in the Deep South to your borders."

Thorr nodded. "Hmmm, a servant woman would not know the term War Terror. We have had Minima traders to my Otaa's Hamlet of Hammer Forge. None of the servants had the refinement of voice you bare. Something tells me you are more than a person of high station. Not a mere servant girl at all."

"You are not as wooden as your brow suggests," said the girl. "And you have manners, not like those from High Keeper Jallanaa retinue who helped the Celeron traders take us.

Thorr pulled back hearing the Keeper's name and insinuated actions. "Hold your tongue. You slander the Keeper's name at great risk. What has mighty Jallanaa's warriors got to do with the crime you speak of? Answer quickly. What do you know?"

The girl looked at him defiant with fire in her eyes.

"How do I know you are not one of the scarzen traitors who would sell their allies for profit?"

"Because if you are Minima, you have the reach skill, yes."

"I do," said the maiden.

"Then you would know how to probe my words for truth or lie. You will, therefore, know I have just spoken without deception. You have also seen me attacked by those who are part of this mischief intending *me* put down. If that is not enough, I could have left you tied for whomever to do with you as they please, or the beasts of these lands to gnaw on your bones. Instead, I am trying to help. I ask again, what is your name?"

The girl straightened her back and considered the scarzen's face.

"I am Princess Nattai, sister to Queen Yasmin ruler of the Minima and Master at Arms for Her Majesties guard."

Thorr's expression crimped. "That is a high claim. If true, whoever wrote your protocols needs reprimanding."

"I wrote those protocols, stone head," snapped Nattai. "I had a plan. Things were working out fine 'til a trusted informant switched sides. After that, things turned sour and didn't go as I liked."

"Your educators were clearly inferior," said Thorr. "You should have consulted with the lawbreakers in the extreme to recover your lost honor."

"Hey, Big Brows! Let's do the *how I messed up* sarcasm dance later! Set us free now! If you provide escort to my Queen's stronghold she will reward you justly, you have my word as a Minima officer. There you shall also know the truth of your glorious High Keeper Jallanaa's deceit."

Thorr looked at her shackles and saw they needed a key.

"Where is the release rod for your bonds?"

"On the body of the one you planted in the long grass over there," said Nattai

Thorr looked to where the dead Celeron lay and nodded.

"What do they call you scarzen?" asked Nattai.

"Very well," he said untying her hands. "Remain here," Thorr said ignoring the question.

He stood and walked over to the others. Though disheveled and untidy from their ordeal, none of their injuries looked fatal. Picking them up like sacks of grain in the crook of his arms, he carried them to Nattai and set each one down with care.

"Your hands are free," said Thorr. "Untie the others while I retrieve the key. Keep quiet, there is clan not of my mind about, they will do you harm if you are detected."

Nattai nodded. Thorr stood and walked away a few paces and then turned to look back at her, thinking.

"I am Thorr, offspring of Tralldon, war chief and leader of Hammer Forge clan."

He turned away and left to find the key on the body of the dead Celeron.

Thorr returned a short while later, key in his possession to find the girls all standing waiting for him. He handed Nattai the key that was so tiny in his heavy palm. Nattai unshackled herself and quickly as possible did the same for the others.

"I also found this beside the body of the Wagon Master," said Thorr holding out a shiny metal flask. "To make such a desperate escape with this in hand, he will have known its worth. This is a standard field flask from the pouch of one of our engineers. In reality for any none scarzen to be caught in possession of this unmodified Trilix, means certain death for the possessor and all connected.

The scarzen who gave it to him would have known that. There are many patrols between here and the Celeron boarder. In some hands, this trilix could have earned him a king's ransom in clink."

Nattai looked at the injured girl holding her arm.

"The blue liquid's reputation for rejuvenating of broken limbs is legendary. Can't we use it for Usul's arm?"

"No," said Thorr. "Should this mixture be applied to her skin, one drop would ensure a death swift and, um, most volatile."

Nattai considered their big rescuer's actions carefully. "So you really do intend helping us. I saw one of the scarzen give it to the Wagon Master as payment saying; *that his help in their agenda should be justly rewarded.* They also said my value as ransom, in particular, would be most prized by their superior."

Thorr looked at her and the other girls thinking hard. Little could be read by his outward expression. Then he looked at the silver flask. "It bears the embossed seal of Talon South. There is only one way he could have acquired it."

Looking past Thorr he saw the woman's face turn scarlet with anger. "Perhaps it was them," said Nattai looking past him.

She lifted her nose to draw his attention away in the distance behind. Thorr turned to see the threat. He slid the trilix flask into an empty utility slot on his basic issue battle belt. In the mid-distance, he saw two scarzen approaching in plain view clearly fixated on them. He recognized one of them instantly.

Morlaak. Jallanaa's unit leader from Hammer forge. How they could have tracked me so quickly, he wondered in frustration. "Are they the ones who helped take you captive?" he asked Nattai.

"Yes," she said. "I recognize the one on the left with the dark chest armor and war axe."

"His name is . . ."

"Morlaak," they both said audibly.

Suddenly three more scarzen uncloaked behind the advancing two. In a matter of steps, they had all formed a full battle circle with Morlaak moving to the center as battle consult coordinator.

"That Morlaak is the cause of our grief, and the one I have a score to settle with most."

"I am their prime interest," said Thorr.

"Not according to the amount of clink they were being paid to sell me and my unit into slavery," said Nattai. "I'll not be a prisoner again."

"Their formation and demeanor do not suggest a disposition for take-and-hold," said Thorr. He looked at Nattai "Time for you to leave, now."

"You can't take on five warriors by yourself," said Nattai.

"I was bred to take on much worse and you will not see tomorrow if I don't. You must report the crime against you."

Without explaining further, Thorr turned and shepherded the other woman swiftly to the last wagon. With one arm and a focused field of kin in his palm, he swept all the heavier supplies off the back of the tray. A bundle of possessions spilled to the ground. With the other discarded articles Nattai recognized something of hers. Thorr began picking the girls up hurriedly plonking them on the vacant wagon tray.

"This is madness," said Nattai her voice showing signs of stress. "Your death will achieve nothing."

"If it is honorable, the ancestors will disagree with you," said Thorr moving swiftly from one task to another.

He reached a hand out for Nattai to put her on the wagon. She evaded his grasp and raced for her belongings. Tossing some things aside she was clearly looking for something in particular.

"Stop! There is no time for parley," said Thorr. "Those approaching will end you in ways that make Ludd's earth demons squeamish."

"Who said anything about intending a parley," said Nattai. Standing with a couple of articles in hand she hurried back to Thorr's position. "They best be ready to earn that victory."

In one hand Nattai held an elegant laminated gilded short bow. She'd slung a quiver of arrows over one shoulder.

"This is foolish. Do as I command," Thorr snapped. "Take this wagon, save your allies."

"You don't command me Big Brows. I make a stand where I must. Besides, I outrank you. You here to argue or kick the shak out of *them?*" asked Nattai jutting her jaw at the oncoming enemy.

Thorr looked to the coming threat. They had not begun to form a battle circle or charge. Their confidence in number and ability for the exchange was clear by their steady unified advance.

They think us no challenge, he thought. *Good, we have a chance. "What do you have in mind?"* he asked Nattai swinging his view to her.

She tossed the quiver to the ground and pulled a handful of arrow shafts from within.

"They have no heads! How will you use them to bite the enemy?" asked Thorr.

"No, they don't, but . . ." she turned the head of a ring on her center finger right side up. Thorr saw the ring was set with a jewel in the form of a red star.

Nattai reached into the quiver again and pulled another arrow from within not visible before.

"What is that?" he asked. "I have never seen an arrow like that before. Is it made of ice?"

"No. We call it a ghost arrow. It is a Minima bow's finest accompaniment. It's invisible unless used by an archer wearing this ring." Nattai wiggled her finger. "It's also the one thing neither your power of kin or armored skin can repel. She knocked the arrow. It won't be seen, but it will be felt."

Revealed by the power of her ring, the shaft indeed looked made of clear ice. A broad black warhead one end, and onyx fletching on the other, it was clearly an arrow not intended to be withdrawn once it's target had been bitten.

"You expect a victory with one shaft?"

"I expect to buy time," said Nattai. "Go to our Queen, *may she prevail.* Overland, you are much faster than any horse. Tell them what you have seen. Tell of the High Keeper's and his rogue scarzen unit's involvement in the slavery."

"I will be more effective reporting such a crime to the Master at Arms at Talon West," said Thorr.

"No, we must be careful implicating Jallanaa. My queen will have both power and persuasion to bring them to trial." "You're aware Keeper Jallanaa and our Queen rarely see eye to eye."

"Such privileged news does not reach the firesides of our outpost. But this treachery is evidence of why such is possible."

"It's true, we don't want a border war. Good sense on both sides will see an investigation with due diligence."

"Why are scarzen always so stubborn, very well, she said," and snapped a glance his way then looked to the girl driving the wagon. "Juna, tell our Queen of this one's honor and courage to help us."

"I will," said the girl.

"Time to go," said Thorr.

Nattai looked to the driver. "Do you know the south trail?"

"Yes," said the driver frowning with flushed cheeks. "Princess, don't let this be your end."

Nattai looked at Thorr. "We can do this can't we, Big Brows?"

Thorr looked at her and nodded with a grunt of agreement.

"Then, you shall have all the support I can provide before I follow my allies," said Nattai.

Thorr made two fists activating his buckler impalers.

"I am only a pup in the eyes of many," he said looking to their approaching enemies. "I have no status worthy of consulting with them. They are seasoned veterans." Thorr looked at each of the girls. "But by the ancestors, Thorr of Hammer Forge shall bar their way. They will know misery for what they have done."

"You're much more than what they bargain for Big Brows," said Nattai. "Show them the full measure of your strength." Nattai focused on the wagon driver. "Turn this crate around Juna and go. Don't look back, I'll join you later."

The driver's expression showed she disagreed, but she nodded and slapped the team with the reins. The wagon jolted forward forcing everyone to grab for a secure hand hold. In a small cloud of dust the wagon rumbled away in a U-turn.

"Stop for no-one, 'til you reach our border outpost!" Nattai shouted.

As the wagon straightened up on its escape path, Juna whistled and whipped the reins. The team burst onward into a full gallop with the passengers hanging on desperately.

Watching the wagon shrink in the distance amidst a cloud of dust, both Thorr and Nattai looked to each other.

"They will find fewer scarzen patrols on that border road," said Thorr.

"If they remember to take the right fork," said Nattai.

They turned to stand against their enemy Nattai beside Thorr.

"What now then willful sister?" asked Thorr.

Nattai's expression turned grim. "Now let's make them earn their victory." She marched two deliberate steps forward in front of Thorr. Facing their enemy she notched an arrow and drew her bow to full strain. "Let me make it plain then".

Taking deliberate aim at the scarzen advancing on their right flank she loosed her arrow. The war bolt sped away with an air ripping zip and a gentle spin over one the hundred paces. It struck the intended target hard almost passing through the neck. Her mark's steps faltered and then stalled. They grasped the shaft of the arrow in their throat with both hands before plunging forward dead with a thud, face-planting into the dirt.

The remaining four scarzen stopped, looking at their fallen ally.

Thorr slung her a glance. "Stugat! Nice shot little sister. Do you have another?"

"No, I only had one Ghost Arrow left," said Nattai.

"You have stones little sister. That one certainly has his cooler well kicked."

"I was aiming for his face," said Nattai. "Why have the others stopped?"

The scarzen that had seemed to be issuing the orders from the rear had the attention of the others and made some hand gestures plane to see.

"Ignore the ruse of the hand signals," said Thorr. "Scarzen in units this size converse mind to mind."

Just as Thorr's words finished, they all turned to face him and Nattai again.

"You have evened the odds little sister. Only four against one now." Thorr looked to one of the remaining teams idly standing by. Thorr moved hastily to the lead horse and casually snapped the harness, freeing it from the rest of the team. He looked over his shoulder to Nattai. "Come, your strength in this consult is at an end. Take this mount, protect your clan. I will draw them away north."

"I should stay. I can help,' said Nattai.

"All you will do is die for no good reason," said Thorr. "You're more useful to your Queen alive than dead. Make your escape now!"

Nattai looked at him reluctantly. "Good luck Big Brows, we'll meet again." She bolted for the horse.

Thorr watched Nattai approach and skillfully leap to her mount's back taking a fist full of mane. She gave the horse a jab in the ribs with her heels and it bolted. With a clatter of hooves, the horse galloped off. A feeling of impending doom forced Thorr to turn all his focus on the enemies drawing near. He sprinted for his travel sack. Snatching it up by its strap, he slung it over his right shoulder on the run and charged off as fast as his legs would carry him. The leading pair of enemies opened the consult by hurling apple sized silvery kinetic repel fields over his head. Thorr knew each one had the capacity to put him on his back.

"Stand and be accountable," one of them bellowed.

Thorr ignored the order. Instead, he looked back flicking his chin with his fingertips in open insult goading them to pursue. He cut right wanting the four remaining scarzen to follow, only three did. One of them broke away giving chase in Nattai's direction.

CHAPTER

6

Galloping Hope

Head down and long auburn locks flying astride her galloping mount, Nattai rode her mare with the skill of a true Luddlian horse master. Free of its harness and wheeled burden, her horse's strong legs and hooves pounded the ground with a determined charge. Up she rode making a steady ascent east along a forested slope trail. She held on using the remains of the harness still around its broad shoulders. The fading image of the racing wagon churned a ball of dust in the distance. Knowing they may well be followed, Nattai slowed her mount's pace looking for an alternate route. She spied a steeper ascending path right into the tree line and left the road behind. Using her knees to hold on, Nattai reached down and tore off a piece of her dress's white linen under sleeve. She snagged it over a branch she passed in plain view, intending any would-be pursuer drawn away from the slower wagon's direction. Having a strong affinity with animals, Nattai's mount responded to its rider as if the two had been bonded for life. Instinctively the mare avoided treacherous foot falls and remained steady under her confident rider's direction. They charged up and along a natural wilderness corridor following a well-trodden trail. Checking over her left shoulder, Nattai shivered with the shock of seeing her lone pursuer closing in. It caused her to draw a steadying breath. The scarzen made no attempt to conceal their advance. The pressure of their menacing approach and impending doom forced her mount's speed to the limit. Nattai knew it wouldn't be long before her horse must slow by half or die. She also knew a scarzen could maintain their present stride for a full day and more without rest. They had two hearts to depend on. She also knew once caught, the scarzen would ruthlessly execute both her and the horse before getting rid of the evidence. She began looking for a faster way down, checking back now and then for her pursuer, but the scarzen was gone. She checked high and right and saw to her terror that the warrior had taken the higher ground and begun to turn for a downhill assault.

How did they get up there so fast? Her mind raced.

Leaning forward, the scarzen started their downward charge intending to end their prey. Nattai urged more from her mare as a wave of fear took hold of them both. Her horse gave all that was left. Legs driving him full sprint downhill, Nattai's scarzen pursuer hurled a repel barrier at her. She felt it's cold burn speed passed her ear, and then saw it twisting and speeding its way forward as a destructive silver teardrop. The barrier struck the base of a coarse-barked tree that grew out over the trail on the high side of the bank. A cutting spray of wood chips startled her horse and it balked with a fearful whinny reluctant to proceed. Wrestling to keep the animal pointing forward Nattai fought with the horse's determination to about face and charge straight into the waiting arms of the warrior assassin. She saw the tree had remained standing though it foundation was damaged. She dug her heels into the horse's ribs none too gentle. Her mount lunged forward again bolting past the tree in an unrestrained adrenaline charged gallop. Nattai urged her horse down the slope to a narrower lower track. Now she could hear the pounding footfall of her pursuer wanting to finish her. The approaching heavy steps made her heart race. She dared not look back, lest the sight of her enemy's closeness destroyed her will to go on.

Behind her, the scarzen landed upon the trail Nattai had just left. Without missing a step he burst forward into an aggressive sprint seeing their target guide her animal skillfully down the slope. The scarzen raced along toward the tree his barrier had just struck following her same line. Through the forest, the wind suddenly picked up and the tree that has threatened Nattai's advance began to plummet downward causing the scarzen to leap high to clear the obstruction. The tree came down with a crash across the path, branches splintering and throwing debris in a rising cloud of gray dust. The scarzen's powerful jump of twice his own height and the arc of his descent easily cleared the obstruction. Gravity and an uncontrollable descent guided his landing to a patch of Grey Shale, which gave way to his weight immediately. As if he'd landed in a pool of thick soup, the earth swallowed him whole with a *plonk* and the assassin was gone.

Further down the slope, Nattai and her horse picked their way toward the bottom. In its haste, the horse slipped more than once. Nattai felt at any moment she would meet her end. Her deadly pace did not stop until they burst from the tree line to arrive on the eastbound road below. There she stopped her horse's body slick with white sweat. She knew her mount was spent. She jumped off and looked back up the slope preparing to face her end. But there was no eight-foot tall instrument of death to be seen. No sound of steps to be heard. Only a crisp breeze to rattle the branch of the trees above suggested any sign of movement. Her feeling of impending doom began to wash away. Her enemy was . . . gone.

"What just happened?" she asked aloud talking to her horse.

The animal snorted and shook its head. Then, on the breeze in the distance, Nattai thought she heard a sinister laugh. The whisper of . . . *soon freedom comes,* sent a chill down her spine, and then the wind dropped leaving only total silence. After moments passed, she climbed aboard her mount once more. She patted the animal on the neck.

"Come on noble beast, as you have done for me, I will look after you now. But we must catch the wagon I pray is charging toward our border.

Nattai urged her mount onward.

CHAPTER

7

Countermeasures

Thorr couldn't know if Nattai had made good her escape as he charged through ever thickening tall fan grass and scrub. She had shown real courage back at the wagons and he had felt a strange connection to her that puzzled him. But being pursued by even one unyielding scarzen assault warrior meant her chances of survival were slim. As he crashed his way through the underbrush, clouds overhead supported the bleak circumstance shifting to a stormy blue-gray hue. A stiff chilling wind picked up pressing against Thorr's face. It felt like some unseen cold hand pressed to slow him down. On the horizon, thunder rumbled and a hint of chain lightning crossed the sky. He fled leading his *own* lethal pursuers into the boulder-littered belly of the nearby forest's steep-sided gully. Thorr's concern for Nattai's safety clung to him more than his own need for survival.

Ancestors favor her, he told himself.

Dodging one large hump of moss covered stone and heavy fallen branches, Thorr shot a look back over one shoulder. Those hunting him were no longer pursuing in a cluster. Instead, they had spread out into what he knew was an attack formation.

They are making ready, he thought.

One chased him from in full view directly behind. It was the unit commander, Morlaak long knife in hand. He saw Morlaak wave his free arm forward as if swimming and from his hand shot a large silver teardrop of kin energy about the size of a melon. As it sped toward Thorr with the fluttering sound of a speeding stone he ducked his head just in time for the blistering projectile to miss him by a hand span.

"Stop, deserter!" Bellowed Morlaak. "Stand and accept Keeper Jallanaa's justice!"

Justice! He had seen their justice.

Having no intention of being tried and executed on the spot, Thorr snapped his view forward and charged on. With the others nowhere to be seen, Thorr knew they had activated their blur skill to blend in with their surroundings. They were hunting silently.

Likely moved to the steeper flanks. That is what I would have done, he thought.

Another hurled a kin repel field. The blast struck and glanced off his shoulder, its percussive force wrong-footed him for several steps. The kin field finished its trajectory crashing against a large stone. A spray of sharp stone shards and debris peppered his face as he sprinted by.

"Don't make it harder than it needs to be," shouted Morlaak. "Come on Broz, accept your circumstance. We'll give you an honorable transition worthy of the ancestor's acceptance!"

As an ardent student of scarzen war strategy, Thorr knew what Morlaak's ruse was intended to do. If he slowed in any way, a claw assault would soon follow to end the matter. Thorr knew his pursuers would treat him like any of Ludd's apex predators, delivering a swift and cunning execution. But, hunting one of their own sentinels, even though he was an un-battle tested pup, still required caution. That was now to *his* advantage. They had seen him consult with one of their own earlier, with a very unexpected outcome. A light rain began to fall.

Racing forward with both hearts pumping at full strength, Thorr sprang over the thick girth of a fallen tree trunk. Landing in the wet underbrush on the other side with a thud, his powerful legs drove him on. Deliberately he searched ahead for a hide-and-ambush position.

"Need to use their caution against them," he told himself.

Then he spied a broad red angular boulder some short strides ahead.

"There".

Throwing himself in behind it, he waited. Drawing his right arm buckler back for a full swing Thorr set his footing to lunge and deliver a single devastating blow. Although mere seconds behind and bearing down on Thorr's position tenaciously, Morlaak had lost momentary sight of his much larger opponent between stone and shadows. Thorr's keen ears measured Morlaak's closing steps. Instinct to move took over. Thorr turned into the oncoming sprinter's path and swung toward them at the same time.

The power in the crook of Thorr's arm met Morlaak in the neck with overwhelming impact. The shocking power of the blow swept Morlaak's feet from under him. His head fell back while his body carried forward, which flipped him, arse-over-head with a gut-wrenching crash and groan. Thorr needed only two strides to be standing over him.

He watched Morlaak attempt to role to his feet and lift his long knife still gripped. Thorr stepped in with one heavy lift of his shin and boot into Morlaak's chest. Bones were heard to crack with the impact and Morlaak gasped in pain. The strength of the kick hurled Morlaak backward against a stone shoulder where he struck his head leaving him slumped near unconscious. Thorr stepped in and took Morlaak's discarded blade laying on the ground a short stride away. He then bolted for the shadows in a northerly direction for Talon West.

∗∗∗

Morlaak's subordinates soon found him propped against the base of the stone. He was conscious. One hand partly covered a bleeding injury over one eye.

"Raxx, do a perimeter search," ordered the shorter of the two warriors. He stood there with a crescent moon blade in one hand still expecting to consult. "See if the criminal is still close by. If you encounter them, ensure the consult is short and final."

Raxx acknowledged the command with a salute. Eyes down he presented his right cheek in a passive gesture. He applied his blur skill and moved off into the shadows to begin his search. The remaining warrior looked at his commander who he recognized was in some substantial pain. Seeing Morlaak clutching his free arm in against his ribs, he knelt down next to Morlaak to give aid.

"Sir, are you alright?"

Morlaak pulled a hand away covering his forehead to reveal a nasty gash suffered in the fall. He tried to reposition himself and winced in discomfort. The subordinate attempted to wipe Morlaak's fringe of fine braids away to inspect the wound. Morlaak brushed his hand aside.

"Leave it," he snapped.

"Sir, if I don't treat that wound, the rot will soon set in. Fever will surely follow. I see your ribs are damaged too by the way you hold your side. Are you broken there? If you are, you will not be able to travel swiftly or consult at full capacity."

Sourly, Morlaak looked at the other scarzen. "Treat me if you must."

His reply came in his usual unsettling soft cold tone.

The warrior leaned forward to examine the wound again. Morlaak grabbed his wrist with a blood covered palm.

"No scar residue will be tolerated, understand. Circumstance will not lean in your favor if such exists. I'll not have my face detail whispered about in the taverns."

"The trilix I carry is first-grade, Sir," said the warrior. "It is from High Keeper Jallanaa's personal stockpile. No suggestion of error will remain."

Morlaak frowned in disapproval.

"Are you insinuating my consult with a pup lacked standards and dignity befitting my station?"

"No, Sir I . . ."

"Let the Blue do its work and Hoxxaa's hand bless your efforts. Then I want that Broz's head in a bag so I can shak down their neck. No one disrespects Morlaak with a cheap shot like that and remains standing."

Morlaak's subordinate pulled a trilix flask from his utility belt to treat the gash zig-zagging down Morlaak's forehead. He pulled a piece of wadding from a metal sleeve on the side of the flask and uncorked the top. The warrior gave the flask a short shake holding with the wadding over its mouth. He suddenly stopped, his expression turning to puzzlement. He applied the first treatment to Morlaak's head, then hesitated.

"Why am I waiting?" asked Morlaak.

"Ah . . . apologies, Sir. My flask is all but empty. After his attempt to chastise our quarry, I used the majority of my trilix trying to revive High Keeper Jallanaa's nephew, Solaak. But his brains were crushed flat from the impact of the pup's impressive blow. Even a near full flask of Trilix wouldn't revive him."

"Grrr, don't raise the criminal up you beetle brained Broznick," snapped Morlaak. "I saw what the Sentinel Pup did! Don't kid yourself. He only received aid for a moment by an ancestor out for a lark. Shack, here," Morlaak tried to reach for his personal flask with a free hand. "Use mine." But the flask was gone. "Ahh, must have lost it in the encounter. Don't just stand there with your face looking slapped, look around broz. It must be nearby. My consult occurred over there, next to that stone shoulder."

Morlaak's subordinate complied and went across to search. He returned some moments later with a flask in hand. Morlaak smiled.

"Good. Now get on with it. We have a criminal to bring to heel."

Morlaak looked down to undo the clips holding his drommal-hide chest and torso armor in place. About to expose his rib injury for treatment, he stopped realizing the other warrior still stood at a distance. He looked at the other scarzen again.

"Well, don't just stand there as if you've shacked yourself. Come on, apply the Trilix."

The warrior held up Morlaak's flask minus its lid like someone who had just lost a sure bet.

"Your flask's lid was nowhere to be found, Sir. Its Trilix ration is exhausted too. I have enough in mine to treat your face or your ribs, not both. Which shall I tend too?"

Morlaak angst over the decision for a brief time.

"Treat my face you fool.

The warrior approached Morlaak and applied the last of his Trilix to Morlaak's injury. Swiftly, the swelling reduced and the wound closed leaving only a fading blue hue where the injury once stood. The aiding warrior nodded with satisfaction and stood back for his commander to get to his feet.

"He is a pup, Sir. What more trouble could he possibly unleash on us?"

Morlaak re-secured the tabs on his torso armor.

"From recent examples scout, obviously quite a lot."

"Tuaak will have him chased down swiftly. Probably heading back with his head in a bag as we speak. We could make camp here and await his return. Give your ribs time to settle."

Morlaak stepped toward to the warrior.

"Why don't *we* trek north a little to meet him, just to be sure, hmm," said Morlaak sarcastically and led the way forward.

***

At full pace, Thorr had tried to put as much distance between himself and the others. Unfortunately for him, the grace of the ancestors in his favor didn't hold, and the swifter scarzen scout sent on to track him made their intercept at the fork of a natural gully. On slopes of that lonely, nameless place, amidst a tangle of fallen trees, their encounter proved sudden and brutal. Blood was spilled on both sides. They had struggled furiously, the smaller and more experienced warrior used all his battle experience to end the troublesome interloper. But his zeal to end the matter suddenly ended him instead. The full length of Thorr's impaler skewered him from clavicle to base of abdomen puncturing both his hearts.

Thorr bent at the knees and with a colossal wave of one arm, hurled the dead body high into the branches of a close by tree. There the body snagged in a fork.

Nursing a deep knife wound to his left arm and weakened from the ordeal, Thorr was forced to move on leaving his fallen adversary in plain view.

He'd made his way to the next ridge to the edge of a growing forest of red-barked Banjaak trees. There he thought to use the Trilix he carried as evidence. Severe pain mounting, reluctantly, he reached for the flask on his belt. Softly to his left, a breeze blew through the bronze yellow leaves in the forest. With their fluttering, he thought he heard someone speak.

"It will mean your end."

Thorr stayed his hand, thinking. He looked for the speaker ready to deal damage the best way he could. But there was no one to be found. He relaxed and thought on the using the trilix again.

Hmm, breaking the seal could see me incriminated too, he thought.

Holding his wounded arm with his other hand he stopped. With gentle hills folding into one another away to the distance, he tried to gage direct north and shook his head.

"Where am I?" he muttered.

This part of Scarza was completely unfamiliar to him. With late afternoon settling in, Thorr looked skyward for the glimpse of early stars. Gray cloud cover and steady rain obscured his view, so he went to his next option to find a way forward. Delving into the archives of his memory, Thorr began to recall the traditional Moosaak or *song lines* of his clan. The Song Lines in rhyme and fable had offered landmarks, shelter and provisions across Scarza to travelers for generations.

Unlike bunker-born warriors of present Scarza who had relinquished such practice in preference of physical maps recorded in Chicaa, the old Moosaak ways of navigation were still preferred by Outland clans. Hammer Forge orators had remained a hub for such skills.

"The way forward is in a warrior's head," the pups of Hammer Forge were all told repeatedly. Each piece of Moosaak was loaded typically with double meanings. A deliberate security measure that only those who had the correct verbal keys could unlock. Thorr's Otaa, Tralldon, represented a long line or masterful song line orators and had drilled his pupils well. Thorr had shown an uncommon flair for the subject and committed quite an archive of information

to memory. The surroundings he now stood in invoked a song line memory from this region as he considered the subject of North bearing as a song line came to mind.

From Hammer Forge by North East to the Shale Hills, march the turn of one sun. Then bear North two points for the light of a second day's end till you stand at the edge of the Forest of Shadows. There, Red Banjak trunks in a corridor you'll find, offering safe passage fading north. Travel by east edge to Land Fall's light.

CHAPTER

8

Unlooked for advice

A soaking drizzle pushed by a chilled wind blanketed the thick forest. Drenched, Morlaak and his subordinate picked their way through rarely trodden underbrush pursuing their quarry. With little to no moon this Toran night, travelers would only have their natural vision to depend on. Scarzen fortunately, were blessed with night vision better than most. The ancestors were at least on their side in that.

Annoying night stinging insects enjoyed their fresh blood-filled hosts striking in infuriating waves, heard and felt rather than seen. Morlaak's subordinate felt one of them take a stabbing taste just under his jaw accompanied by a nasty sting. He slapped his neck hard enough to knock a Zukaa cow over and felt the bitten area swell immediately.

Aw, shak!

Morlaak, leading, looked back to the sound momentarily.

"Little Broz almost took my head off," said the warrior.

Morlaak presented a scowl. "Pity. Would have been an improvement," he said and then turned to press on.

Scarzen hardiness aside, navigating the dense forested central region of Scarza had its challenges. Bottomless sink-holes and deceptively treacherous terrain in the hills of the Forest of Shadows had helped many an inexperienced traveler to vanish without a trace. Morlaak had examined his map earlier. He knew this was the forest they now passed through, heading north.

"This can be a dangerous place," he said "Very dangerous.

The only significant landmark between here and Talon West is, he thought a moment, *the outpost of Land Fall. Well, he'll find no aid there.*

"Couldn't we just let the Broz find his way into a sinkhole out here, let Hoxxaa claim him?"

Morlaak ignored the useless verbiage.

"The dangers of traveling at night will encourage even the most determined to stay by their camp fires until dawn. That will buy us time." Morlaak was as stubborn as he was tenacious when his mind was fixed. "This pup has to be stopped before he can speak to any authority about what he has seen."

"None would dare accuse let alone convict a High Keeper of something so low an act as supporting slavery," said his subordinate. "They represent the ancestors."

"It will be my neck for the court martial," said Morlaak. "Then truths twisted to ensure a clear conviction. I'd be found guilty, and the customary humiliating public garroting as penance would follow. Not this scarzen, not this lifetime."

Tracking under such conditions would be a challenge for even the most supremely skilled. Morlaak was a Hunter, the highest qualification a scarzen scout could attain. His tracking skill stood in the realm of exceptional. High Keeper Jallanaa had decorated him personally. Some said Morlaak could find a Black-Blood fly in the dead of night after being blindfolded and thrown off a cliff. Such was his ability to find his target, and this one was going to be found.

That Hammer Forge pup had led them a merry chase, but the wind of advantage was turning in his favor now, he could feel it.

He stopped and turned to speak to his subordinate.

"Bruxx, let me make it simple. If we don't pin the criminal or catch up with our tracker who has dealt with him in another standard hour, we'll make for Land Fall."

"Sir, there is nothing *at* Land Fall. News to our camp yesterday is, Talon West authorities decommissioned the outpost a few days ago. Something about the hot underground stream making the ground unstable. Sinkholes are forming. You spoke about using it as a new route because of the lessoning of patrols in the area."

Morlaak nodded as if agreeing.

"Our simple minded *stone-breaker* won't know that. It's not likely they'll be privy to this region's topography," said Morlaak thoughtfully. "The advantage is ours."

Morlaak pulled a fold of parchment from inside a flap in his armor near his abdomen. With that action, he felt the hot sting of cracked bone shifting and winced uncomfortably. He knelt clamping his arm tight to his ribs. He fumbled with the parchment in one hand and failed to open it.

"Are you alright, Sir? Can I assist?" asked Bruxx.

He gently took the parchment from Morlaak and unfolded it. It revealed a grid map of the central Scarza region that had many landmarks significant to scarzen border tactical defense. Standing, Morlaak looked close to examine the map.

"This is where we last saw him," said Morlaak. "This is the direction he was heading. Hmm, I think this suggests he intends a chance meet with an authority there."

"How can you be certain he would head to Land Fall, Sir?" asked Bruxx in a lowered tone.

"Because it's the only landmark on the map that suggests authority. Our criminal intends to exonerate himself I'd say by pointing blame elsewhere. My guess is he carries evidence of our dealings. Evidence that that twig of a Minima girl, Nattai, will corroborate. Shak! I knew taking her was too much of a risk. She better be pushing up white-petals by now if Tuaak knows what's good for him."

Morlaak glanced at his subordinate who was gaping aloft with a stuck expression not paying attention to his considerations at all. Morlaak sighed.

"I might as well be speaking to stone."

Then Morlaak realized the warrior's gaze had a significance of its own and followed the warrior's focus into the tree canopy.

"Seems Raxx found and consulted with our quarry. He seems to have been ineffective, Sir," said the Bruxx pointing.

There, wedged in a heavy tree fork some thirty feet aloft hung the limp brutally broken body of their comrade.

Morlaak turned his view slowly to his subordinate. "Ya think. Come on weed brain. I know a shortcut. I want that troublesome gate breaker's hearts stopped before sun-up."

CHAPTER

9

Finish the job

Thorr had exited the tree line of the Forest of Shadows without further incident, save one encounter with a hunting pack of Munga spitting web spiders. Tendrils of their silver green web still clung to parts of his body. The altercation had antagonized his weeping injury further. The song line had indeed been accurate. It had guided him to a ridge that overlooked a lower tree canopy to the North West.

"Land Fall should be within sight," he told himself.

Irregular wind blowing through the forest made hearing any enemy approach difficult. Skyward he could see the storm thinning, though rain still fell. A spill of light from both Tora's moons that scarzen song lines taught were *The Eyes of Nur,* lit the way.

He wiped rain spattering his face away with one hand looking hard for his landmark. In the shorter distance, he spied what he'd hoped to find. From a tall spire piercing the canopy flickered a blue flame that commonly marked the position of a scarzen outpost. Feeling relieved, he ignored the pain of his injury. Help would be there, or so he believed. An inner wave of hope welled up inside him spurring him on. He moved down the slope to raise the alarm.

*****

Soon Thorr's steps slowed as he advanced through the woodland. The pain of his injuries forced him to shutdown one of his hearts allowing his internal reserves to replenish. Concerns for Nattai and whether she'd found safety weighed heavy in his mind. A welcome distraction came as some of the old Nur Chronicles rippled through his memory. The song lines taught that the weather was, in reality, the mind of Hoxxaa. If one read the weather correctly, one could know the intent of the coming seasons. Thorr often wondered about the truth in that. He'd heard the wind whisper to him time and again for most of his life. If there was great intelligence behind the seasons' coming and going, he felt no benevolence in it. The voice he heard had something sinister behind it, manipulative and cunning. As he'd always done, he chose to ignore it and go his own way. Something in its intent made him very uneasy.

Something the others never felt at all. Perhaps I'm becoming addled.

His Otaa Tralldon always described Thorr's experiences as a blessing of the ancestors. But Thorr never felt that was quite right. Another clan elder told him once the voice on the wind was a prophecy. They said that Thorr's life would not travel as others did. According to them, Hoxxaa intended Thorr to be an envoy to explore faraway worlds beyond imagining. He never told anyone about that. His gut instincts told him, Hoxxaa's plan for him was something quite different and not in Thorr's best interests. In fact, he hated being out when Hoxxaa was in a bad mood. Hearing Hoxxaa shout his displeasure from amidst the clouds always unsettled Thorr.

There is always trouble when he does this, he thought.

"The Nur chronicles say; *dire strife is expected if Hoxxaa shouts from the clouds. Look for his head in a coming storm. If one knows what to look for, one can know where to avoid disaster.*

Thorr looked aloft to the moons showing their presence through a break in the angry clouds. He sniffed the air.

"Hmm, if that is so," Thorr thought, "this night bears ill will to any wanting to cross Scarza's face. There are no safe lodgings."

He marched on, and it didn't take long before he stood on the outskirts of Land Fall Outpost. In the mid-distance, he could see the front entrance clearly. It was now late, and things around the scarzen outpost showed little obvious activity.

There'll be eyes looking beyond the walls alright, and likely patrols outside too, he thought. *That's how our outpost works at Hammer Forge. Something feels off here, though. How should I approach the gate at this time of night and be certain I am not walking into the arms of my enemies?*

Protocol said he should approach the front gate without deviation in clear view, weapons sheathed. To do otherwise would invoke a pacification order by the outpost security. Engrained discipline told him to march on down and announce himself. But his stronger instinct for trouble held him in place. Thinking, he remained still. It was just a feeling, a bad feeling. His eyes swept the area from left to right and back again.

He looked in vain for possible signs of hidden defenses as his view swung again to the front gate. At ground level, spaced some thirty paces apart, black resin-soaked timbers burned in braziers. Each hot spot splashed a wash of soft yellow light that bled into a shadow some paces out. The braziers highlighted the defense wall's line stretching away in both directions curving out of sight. The rain stopped, and a gentle breeze ruffled the brazier's flames. The effect caused shadows to dance on the wall behind.

"They'll burn even in a soaking rain till dawn," he told himself.

Thorr noted the structure centered in the scarzen-made clearing. It boasted a moat of open ground around the entire outpost, standard for scarzen small structure defenses. A miniature of a full sized scarzen bunker, the outpost's circular defense wall carved from traditional glass-stone stood some twenty feet high. A central keep featured a rising spire at the top battlements as an imposing focal point. He estimated it would be some fifty-five sentinel marching paces from the front gate to the cleared scrub forest edge where he stood.

That's a lot of open ground to cover, he thought.

He suddenly noticed a single figure sitting just inside a sandstone block-built surround that enshrouded the outpost's front gate. The figure inside it presented more as a shadowy outline than in any real detail. Opposite them, a hanging lamp swung gently back and forth, seemingly pushed by a breeze. The lamp light's swing created shifting shadows in the gateway entry. *Maybe a deliberate attention getter?* To the back, next to the figure, stood the heavy metal-strapped door that would usher the way in.

The guard looks as though they could easily be asleep, not, thought Thorr.

Thorr knew this passive scene to be an illusion. His Otaa had instructed Hammer Forge security to do similar things. Somewhere within reach, there would be a cord or pressure plate. When used it would alert security inside to approaching activity. Land Fall fell under High Keeper Jallanaa's jurisdiction, and, as a Hammer Forge clan citizen by default, so did he. At least until he was beyond the out post's north parameter. Then, the High Keeper of Talon West's jurisdiction took over.

Wish brother Boldaa was here to give some guidance, he thought.

There was no way of knowing how far the darker influence of High Keeper Jallanaa's rogue unit pursuing him reached. He felt the drone of a mild headache and fever setting in as a result of his injuries becoming infected.

"Can't stay out here," he told himself and looked over one shoulder. *The enemy will be closing in.*

The increasing pain of his bleeding wound forced a decision.

Have to get some trilix to heal this, or getting to Talon West will be impossible any time soon.

A breeze blew past him from behind as if gentle hands were pressing him on. Thorr nodded to himself.

"Alright then. Down I go."

Just as he went to step forward, the door next to the figure he'd been watching creaked open. Thorr's stomach lurched with the appearance of another and his steps stalled. A second figure, a warrior that until now who had been completely concealed by shadow nearer to the door, stood as if called. The seated individual that Thorr *had been* observing, didn't move a muscle. Silently, the other revealed individual shuffled their way silently inside leaving the door ajar.

This is feeling worse by the skat, thought Thorr.

A moment later, the still seated one slumped forward as if asleep and then fell limply sideways toward the door. Thorr heard a faint bump as they hit against the shoulder of stone at the door. They then rolled off their seat like a wet corn sack and hit the ground with a thud. Thorr's instincts for impending danger jumped a couple of notches.

"Shak!" he said under his breath.

He looked sharp up to the forward parapet for any increased sentry activity and saw none. Even for a small scarzen occupied sanctuary, things remained deathly quiet. His attention dropped quickly to the door when he saw the second individual return. They picked up the fallen body and pushed it back into position. Someone else from behind the door handed the prop-setter a length of timber, which was used to wedge between the body's armpit and the wall. Then the maker of the illusion stood, steadied the lamp opposite and slipped back inside.

Now, what? Thorr asked himself. *One of our own, dead?* He looked about again for signs of struggle. *I see no sign of siege or assault. Where are all the rest of the dead outpost warriors?"*

He gasped as the realization hit him.

"Murdered!" he muttered. *By who? Could it be my enemies have beaten me here?*

His wound stabbed at him pushing him to seek relief from the worsening pain.

Not long till dawn. Must do something. Perhaps there is trilix on the dead one there. If I could get close enough for a swift search, no, what if it's a trap? There will be eyes on spy holes watching for any contact no doubt.

Thorr had been taught enough of outpost layouts to know the open ground around any of them was a deathtrap. Approaching an entrance from either side meant a swift painful death in one form or another. There were usually markers on flag-stones in chicaa giving step direction to residents and escorts new to an area. He had dug many of the stake and fire pits for Hammer Forge himself. Here, no markers could be seen or had been flipped over to hide the information.

"Why would the flag-stones be rolled unless."

He looked up to the parapet again and saw no activity still. He then attempted to survey the ground before him closely for where the traps might be. In a pattern unique to the commander of this outpost's liking, standard security manual adaptations referred to as... *unpleasant deterrents* would be set. No two approaches the same. One safe way in and out. He thought deeply for any song lines that might help. Nothing useful came to mind. A cold feeling washed over him. Someone had moved in from behind. Calmly Thorr activated the buckler's impaler on his good side ready to act. As the tension of the spring lock in the buckler released, the impaler slid steadily forward with the fine sound of extruding polished metal and click-locked into position.

"You won't need that here," whispered a familiar voice in his Hammer Forge dialect. The interruption made Thorr straighten. Don't move, just listen.

"I'd tread real careful now scarzen! You're between an oncoming thrust and a stone wall. If you don't get out of the way, you won't enjoy the outcome."

The familiar tone of the new arrival stopped Thorr springing to action that would make himself obvious to outpost eyes. He looked sharp left, right and behind for the speaker, but spied no one.

"Where are you?" Thorr demanded in a forced whisper.

"Calm down big fella," his new company replied. "You won't see the end of another sunset if you don't listen to me, right now! So settle down and turn your focus on that front gate. While we have a little chat."

The male voice Thorr heard had a strangely calming effect on him. "You sound familiar. Do I know you?"

"Really, I do? What do you remember exactly?" asked the visitor with keen interest in his tone.

"I remember someone that sounded exactly like you who spoke to me recently, but where and about what is a fog in my thoughts."

Thorr heard movement behind and went to turn.

"Stay where you are. We've had enough complications already this day."

The visitor, accompanied by someone or something drew closer.

"Hmm, that's odd," they said, "very odd. For now, you can call me—Uniss. Does that name sound familiar too?"

"Hmm, maybe," Thorr nodded giving no real sign he had remembered any details clearly that transpired between them earlier.

Then he heard mumbling from the one called Uniss, speaking to someone else. After a short moment, what or who ever it was scurried off into the underbrush. A disquieting sweet smell of decay he'd experienced many times in his life wafted past from the opposite direction.

"That smell means very bad things are about," said Uniss.

"I'll say," said Thorr. Smelling like that, I doubt even an apothecary's stomach-blast potion could aid an ailment that bad."

"Well, at least you still have your sense of humor. Listen, we are a little constrained for time. There is some nastiness about this place with a keen interest in stopping *you* reaching your objective.

"I picked up on that already," said Thorr.

"No, you are only seeing the puppets, not the puppeteer. I'm talking about something, someone more evil than you can possibly imagine, and right now I'm pretty certain it has its eye on you."

"Really. You clearly don't know my Otaa's monster in law, Muxx. She's lethal with a short blade but far worse with her tongue. My Otaa always said . . ."

"Be serious pup!" Uniss snapped. "You're surrounded by some foul business here. If I'm to help you, do as I ask or I'll leave you to your dry wit and deep knife wound for strategic support."

"Sorry," said Thorr humbly. "I've had a disagreeable day."

Thorr did as asked, still listening intently trying to work out where the one calling himself Uniss might be standing.

"Why are you helping me? What do you want?"

"What I want is for you to come out of this alive and to be part of the future you were born to be involved in."

"What are you talking about?"

"A little princess I bumped into back a ways said you might need a hand, and I can see you do. That wound you're carrying is only going to get worse."

"You saw Nattai? She is alright?"

"That's the one. Nattai wanted you to know she made it to safety, thanks to you."

"Did she?"

Thorr wondered quickly if the voice projection was a mind-game of Morlaak. A tactic amongst his race used by some with high Kin ability.

"This isn't a mind game; I'm not lying scarzen if that's what you're wondering. Queen Yazmin is a friend of mine. I was in the area on my way to Talon East when I bumped into the young princess. Said you'd been in quite a difficult place. I've spoken to your Otaa, Tralldon, on matters of importance in the past, and just in the past few hours as it happens too. He gave me the background, said to tell you *Dave* was fine. Said that should be enough to know our contact was real."

"How can you be in so many places so quickly?"

"How I get about is unimportant, that I'm here now is. Let me provide what assistance I can. You need to set things right."

"How will you help?" Thorr asked evenly.

"For starters, we have to get that wound fixed. Talon West is still a long way off. Approaching that front gate direct will not end well for you."

"How do you know?"

"Because a short while ago we witnessed a bit of a skirmish over there. An ambush between brothers you might say while the final departing guard did last rounds. Hence our dead friend at the gate."

"Why? What are you talking about? Are we at war?" asked Thorr an edge of frustration in his tone.

"Your untimely interference has presented your pursuers with a serious dilemma. No one was supposed to be here when they arrived ahead of you. Now there are several dead to be accounted for. Those waiting inside for you intend, after you are silenced, to provide evidence of the murders that will ensure the crime rests squarely on you.

Hearing Uniss's explanation Thorr's shoulders slumped.

"Sorry pup, the place is deserted. Problems with the foundations. It's ready to collapse into a large hole. The departing garrison rigged things inside to be . . . unfriendly to any opportunistic fortune hunters too. But maybe there is a way we can turn this around."

Thorr lifted his head frowning in puzzlement. "How can what you have told me be made a strength in my advantage? I must evade them, attempt to make it to Talon West."

"Ordinarily you'd be right. But by now you're likely experiencing a pretty fierce headache, am I right?" asked Uniss.

"I am still strong," said Thorr.

"Not for long," said Uniss. "You already have the sweating fever growing from that wound, and unless I misjudge the color of that blood seeping from it, it's already turned sour."

Thorr nodded with a wince while holding his wounded side.

"So your strategy is, to let the environment kill you for them?"

"No, of course not."

"Seems that way to me. Look, your Otaa didn't survive as many battles he has by using poor judgment. No, he's a smart one your Otaa."

"Make your point." Thorr snapped.

"Tralldon tells me you have brains more than most scarzen he has ever trained. High praise coming from him."

"He said that?"

"He did. Why don't we use some of them brains instead of your stubbornness, hmm? So you'll have a victory story to tell on your return. Make him proud scarzen, don't be going to your ancestors with a whimper."

"Grrr, a whimper, Thorr of Hammer Forge will never go out with a whimper."

"Then just remember, nothing's as it seems."

Thorr nodded again. "You are right. What shall I do to achieve victory?"

"Spoken like a true warrior! Now as I see it, you can't use the trilix you're carrying as evidence . . ."

"Right," said Thorr.

"So . . . you need the trilix that's inside that outpost to get where you're going. Option one: at least one of the scarzen inside will carry a supply of trilix enough for you to tend your injuries. You take it from them, heal the wound, head off to Talon West and raise the alarm."

"And option two?" asked Thorr.

"Option two. You scramble around in there hoping someone left a stash of trilix behind while they hunt you down, corner you and finally end your days in as undignified a way as possible, then throw your body down a very deep hole."

Thorr took a deep breath and sighed. "Option one is more appealing?"

"Good. Inside look for an opportunity to render one of the unlucky enemies unconscious. Use them. Set a deception, like the one they have for you at the front gate over. Both inside are on borrowed time anyway, so no need to be gentle.

"There are only two inside?"

"To my knowledge. Deal with them and waste no time in getting to Talon West."

"First sensible thing I've heard in a while," said Thorr.

"Usually, there is no obvious back door to an outpost, right."

"Right."

"But there is a secret tunnel for this one that allows defending warriors to leave outposts unseen to ambush an enemy focused on the Outpost walls."

"Then, where is it?" asked Thorr.

"Listen carefully; We scouted this area earlier. Look at the front gate."

"Okay."

"To avoid any nasty surprises, you'll need to skirt around the left wall. Stay a minimum of fifteen strides away to avoid the hazards."

"Got it."

"Just over three-quarters of the way around you'll see a hump of stone and some scrub. On the far side of that is a flat block of stone about the width of your arms wide. You'll find a combination stone lock on its surface. You'll need to use your kin to unlock it. Be mindful it's likely trapped. Times short. Let's get to it."

Thorr felt a touch on his arm and turned toward it.

"Are you coming t . . ." He looked for Uniss in all directions. Hey, where'd you go?"

Uniss had vanished. As Thorr looked back to the outpost, his wound throbbed sharply urging him to get under way. So without further delay, he stepped off toward his next objective as Uniss had instructed. At least now he had a safer way inside, perhaps.

CHAPTER

10

Dark Places Careful Steps

The directions provided saw Thorr find his way to the general location of the secret tunnel unimpeded. Once close to his objective, he began to notice Chicaa inscribed stone markers giving warnings of the traps protecting the North West wall and tunnel entrance. He passed one Razor Boar who had fallen sad victim to an impalement pit. The ugly beast had clearly slipped into the pit in the last moments of a charge or attempt to flee. Several vicious wooden stakes protruded through its chest and neck.

"Unlucky," Thorr said to the dead mammal under his breath.

He advanced, paying close attention to the signs to avoid a similar fate.

He found the described land mark just as the now fading memory of his aid's guiding voice said he would. Thorr stepped in closer and knelt down to examine it. Pulling aside the half-round of a decaying stump, he saw a crafted flat face of stone underneath. He began looking for the signs of a scarzen made entry.

Now much closer to the defense wall too, occasional faint sounds of activity from inside the outpost touched his ears. He looked to the parapet above for signs of activity or unwelcome eyes. Seeing none he went back to work. Before him lay a cluster of scrub and stone about twice the width of his arms spread. He pulled the mess aside making as little noise as possible. The cleared space offered a mason hewn flat surface. He brushed a thin layer of loose dirt away with one hand. Five small perfect circles were revealed. Four of them, just less than the circumference of his palm, were spread in a convex half-moon. The larger fifth circle sat inside them completing the entire symbol. Each circle had a defined seam separating it from the rest of the natural rock. The larger circle had the chicaa symbol of two vertical straight lines for *opening* in its center.

To examine the symbols closer, Thorr stretched out a hand placing thumb and fingertip on each smaller circle. The fit for his hand span was perfect. He applied pressure to them. To his surprise, each circle sank into the stone until his palm was flat against the larger circle. Somewhere deep under the rock, he heard a slipping of stone on stone, and a final *tap*. He looked about waiting for some stairwell or way down to be revealed. Nothing. He looked for any opening on the defense wall only strides away too, but nothing happened there either.

"Now what?" he asked himself under his breath.

Then something reminded him that he somehow had to use his kin ability to activate the door. The use of elemental kinetic manipulation though innate to his kind, was not one of *his* strong points. He was bred to be more of a disassembler of bones and structures by force. He had little in the way of mastery for the arcane subtlety the manipulation of kin required. He looked at the symbols again and suddenly wondered about the larger circle under his palm.

"Hmm. Maybe here," he said aloud.

With his hand in place over the symbols, Thorr dug deep into the reservoir of will inside his core. He then focused all his kin through the hand over the symbols and released a soft vocal resonator   *huucha*. In a synchronized action he shunted the heel of his hand forcefully downward. A puff of dust expelled from under it. In the next instant, the circle under his palm popped an inch or so high. Thorr removed his hand to see the larger stone circle turn a full rotation twice left and one to the right. Somewhere deep underground there was a stone on stone *kur-thunk*. He stood and stepped back. A rectangular seam measuring the size of a small door appeared in the rock. Suddenly it fell away to reveal a stone spiral staircase.

The foulness of what emanated from below made Thorr cover his nose. Was that movement he just heard, or the conspiracy of his mind for dark places? He moved to be squarely positioned to make his way down.

Whatever might be waiting down there, Thorr thought, *is on good terms with most things dead.*

Thorr moved a couple of paces down into the stairwell. His eyes adjusted to the deeper darkness quickly. Further in as he peered downward, soft light from far deeper coaxed him on. Another breath of stale air washed over him along with the smell of burning resin. He took a look over one shoulder where he could see the last vestiges of the night sky through the opening above. Then turning away from the world above ground, he took first steps down toward the dim light and focused on what he might find down there.

The narrow stairwell descended some twenty steps to the next level. When his boot landed on third last step, it dropped another boot-sole thickness under his weight. Some new inner-wall mechanism was set in motion.

Behind him, back up at ground level, he heard what must have been the stone cover concealing the stairwell shunting into action again. Movements finished with a final sound of more sliding stone that locked into place with a dull *voomp*. Thorr tested the step again pressing on it with his boot, and it held fast.

"Well, that's that then," he told himself and moved forward to explore the tunnel.

***

Only a few steps in and Thorr could see the passage was not made for a sentinel's comfort. He had to stoop to step along the partially finished stone worked corridor. It was damper down here too. He'd only traveled some paces around a left curve that instinct told him should point toward the outpost. Then he noticed the formalized stonework leading from the stairwell ended.

"Strange, you'd think the formal stonework would finish from the other direction. Something must have disturbed the mason's efforts."

Light from a low burning side wall lamp nearby showed the walking surface and stone block walls gave way to packed earth and a prop reinforced tunnel.

"Seems no one has topped the lamps up for some time."

He moved to the flickering lamp splashing soft yellow light on the tunnel surfaces. Still wanting to cover his nose from the putrid smell, which seemed to be getting worse he looked closer at the wall.

In the earth and stone surface, he could see horizontal scouring as if some instrument or claw had pushed passed here. No scarzen masonry left marking like this. His blood suddenly ran cold. He propped.

Wait a moment. There's only one thing that was big enough and aggressive enough to dig through Ludd's earth like this. That smell, these markings, the damp tunnel conditions. "Bafaalin," he said aloud with concern.

Bafaalin , a nasty underground invader as the scarzen dubbed it. Bafaalin were at one time rife in the subterranean habitats of Ludd. They had been eradicated from Hammer Forge's subterranean catacombs by his Otaa, Tralldon, and others when their outpost was in its infancy. Thorr was still quite young in those times. Memories of the horrors the hideous worm-like predators inflicted on his clan filtered in. Fatalities most always occurred when a Bafaalin Queen's pit and her larva were ignorantly fallen into. Around Hammer Forge, scarzen frequently broke through a Bafaalin pit wall while following a seam of the precious Trilix blue crystal so highly prized by his race. Some stories from early mystics said Hoxxaa employed them to guard the crystal *before* the scarzen arrived to take over the responsibility. No one apparently told the Bafaalin there'd been a change in management. Hence thick veins of Trilix often meant many hostile Bafaalin.

Thorr remembered his Otutt showing him and his brothers how to prepare a slain Bafaalin Queen for food and other uses. Its anemic white grub body, too big for Thorr to get arms more than half way around could be made into steaks that fed their entire outpost for a full turn of the moons. The tips of the hook-shaped legs of the Queen's under-body served as tools for catching young Jawfish and setting traps. Some member of the consulting party liked to mount a Queen's insectoid face on their walls; his Otaa had two. The Queens spider-like eye clusters were used by scarzen pups who played marbles and Jakjak with them. Thorr had a prize collection passed down over three generations. If there *was* a Bafaalin down here, and by that never forgotten smell there well could be, finding his way out the other side could be difficult.

Humph. Bafaalin, he thought. *If they are still here, it means big trouble.*

Cautiously he moved on.

***

Above ground inside the outpost;

Adjacent to the front gate, a hazard-bag-wall and burning braziers to the right of the outpost's spire. They warned of the edge of a deep sinkhole. The dangerous hazard stretched some sixteen or more large strides from one ragged edge to the other. A black on white sign that said—*limitless fall,* stood in front of the hurriedly placed low wall as a final warning. Uneven foundation cracks at the base of the outpost's three story Whitestone spire drew jagged paths to its solid door frame. They could be clearly seen, marked in red. The damage had caused the structure to lean some 15 degrees to the right, giving the impression it was ready to fall or collapse without warning.

At the west end of the compound, Morlaak and his subordinate hustled to finish the welcome for their expected quarry.

"Are you *sure*, this time?" grumbled Morlaak. "Will the deception stay put? Your sloppy work almost gave the ruse away."

"Yes, Sir," replied his last remaining subordinate setting a trip wire near the western stairwell. "I wedged it in real tight." The subordinate went to say something and hesitated.

"Damn you to the ancestors, what is it now?"

"He was my cousin, Sir. Don't know how I'll ever be able to look his old Otaa in the eyes in coming days."

"Do I look like I give a shak! You'll act the same way I did when I had to remove my Otutt during fourth moon celebrations in days past." Morlaak's subordinate shuffled nervously. "You do it knowing you have a higher purpose Broz. If your cousin was paying attention when we approached the front gate, it would be you painting the earth red now and not them. Now focus getting this mess cleaned up, or looking into the eyes of a tired forgotten warrior like your Otaa will be the least of your concerns."

"Sir?"

"What now?"

"In the north end of the compound, I smelled Bafaalin." The scarzen point in the direction of the escape tunnel. "By the strength of the smell, there is a larva pit close by."

Morlaak looked in the direction indicated. "If we are lucky, the beast will have done our job for us. Now get the rest of those surprises ready for our guest, or I'll throw your sorry arse down that sinkhole over there myself."

***

In the tunnel, cautiously, Thorr made his way along the dim lit tunnel as it continued to bear right. The torches placed at staggered intervals gave his path a sinister feel with several almost out of burning resin. With every step, he focused hard to find the end of the passage. He didn't notice torches some distance behind were now extinguished. At one point a stick cracked under the weight of his boot and broke the silence.

For a moment, he thought he heard a faint scraping noise on the other side of the wall to his right. He placed one cautious hand against the stone surface. Suddenly, the wall section around his hand crumbled and fell dropping rubble at his feet. A hole several times the size of his fist opened. Through it belched a horrid smell. A blink latter something large with fleshy yellow-white skin pressed hard against the wall covering the hole. Thorr pulled back a step feeling a terrible danger within arm's reach. Then, for a few short moments an ominous silence set in and whatever it was moved away from the portal shaped opening. Morbid curiosity pushed Thorr forward to stoop and look through the hole. Light from the other side provided the space's detail and revealed a subterranean chamber.

"What in the name of the ancestors is this?"

It was more than just a manifestation of the natural world. The portion of the chamber he could see had been made with highly skilled mason's hands to form the stone-tiled walls. The space took its light from somewhere unseen above. Thorr had never seen such brilliant unnatural white light before. Then he noticed a concentration of focused light on an object standing against the far wall. In those brief moments, Thorr's expression shifted from confusion to wonder.

"What is that?" he muttered to himself.

The object, a large rectangular rusting green metal box stood easily tall as his sternum. Its appearance was so alien to him, it made his thoughts stall as to what its use could be. The object had many blinking crystals of several colors. They were all arranged above a shelf set no higher than Thorr's knees. Below that, a bank of circular illuminated discs displayed shifting lines and shapes.

Who built that thing?

The noises the object emitted sounded to him like a cluster of warbling birds. His moment of fascination shattered when the ground shuddered under foot. The shock forced him to reach for the wall to steady himself. His attention snapped back to the very real danger of the life form looming within.

Bafaalin! How big?

Behind him, large stone fragments began to fall from the roof and walls. Thorr shot a look behind to see the huge bulging girth of one of Tora's living subterranean terrors smash through the wall only steps away. His eyes widened with the shock and urgency to know of just how big the leviathan was. Another shudder from the stone all around told him all he needed to know and nearly heaved him to the ground. The Bafaalin's ugly orange head rolled through the widening gap in the wall facing directly at Thorr.

A Queen. And a Queen means . . .

His view dropped sharply to the ground near her.

"Oh Shak!"

There, spreading like a pool of silver mucus under her body pooled her larva, and they were moving in his direction. Not just thousands of little versions of her, but hungry little instinctive versions that sought out living organic matter. A Bafaalin Queen's Carvaa, her most revolting and insidious weapon. Suddenly, next to him, under the weight of his pressing arm more of the wall fell away and he almost toppled inside. He struggled to recover his footing. The Bafaalin's serpent-like hiss of aggression raised Thorr's adrenalin as her many-eyed head and body swung toward him. The ground quaked under the weight of her movement. Without warning the ground gave way. A cavernous sinkhole opened swallowing nearly half the chamber's floor area including the strange blinking metal box. It fell into the chasm with its sounds diminishing plummeting away with no crash of hitting bottom heard. The Bafaalin rolled into and nearly filled most of the tunnel with her girth. The silver pool dripping from her orange insectoid face advanced before her as a creeping mass. Thorr grabbed one of the burning lamps and hurled it to ground a short distance in front of him. The spread of flame halted the progress of the Bafaalin's larva. She put her scraggly bearded chin down near the flame and withdraw quickly like a hand touching hot metal. Then she began compressing herself to lunge.

"Shak, she's charging!"

Straightaway Thorr turned to race hard for the end of the tunnel. He sped around the curved corridor hoping there would be an exit soon in sight. He could feel her crashing along through the tunnel in pursuit. Some desperate strides on and he could make out the beginnings of a stairwell cavity ahead leading up.

"Oh no!"

Ahead, Thorr saw a strong dark metal gate recessed in the stairwell barring his way. As the walls and ceiling behind him continued to collapse, he charged at the door for all he was worth. Near striking range, in his last steps at full sprint, Thorr dropped one shoulder toward the obstruction barring his way. With a skip of a step and war cry his Otaa would have been proud of, Thorr summoned all his strength and side-kicked the gate. His boot rammed so hard against the latch plate situated at hip height on the door's right, that the gate exploded outward. The force of the strike hurled the gate up into the stair alcove with a great clatter of metal against stone. Thorr tripped over the backward sliding gate and scrambled to his feet through the gap and up the stairs to escape.

At the top of the stairs, the way out was obstructed by another metal plate flip door. With a roar, Thorr dropped his shoulder again and charged with all his weight. The force of his charge shattered the door lock bolt. The door burst open with such an almighty metallic clang that his exit would have been heard all the way to Talon West. Finishing his charge inside of the outpost compound, Thorr turned sharply and slammed the metal plate door shut again desperate to stop what was on his heels following. He staggered back and fell to the ground lungs and both hearts pounding. Eyes wide he stared at the gate waiting to see if it was safe. The rumblings and earth shudder underfoot subsided into an eerie silence, and he breathed a sigh of relief.

Rolling onto his side about to get to his feet, Thorr looked across the compound. There to the right of the spire striking an arrogant pose hands on hips looking straight at him, stood Morlaak.

"Well you make a grand entrance, I'll give you that pup," said Morlaak shaking his head. "Right on time. All that running about. I wish I had that sort of excess stamina." Morlaak's expression turned grim. "You made me chase you pup; that's got to cost you extra. Your end will be slow and without dignity. Game's over Broz, time to send you on to the ancestors."

CHAPTER

11

Please, Just Die

Still on his side, Thorr stared at Morlaak defiantly. Morlaak advanced with an arrogant stride.

"Thought you would have finished your pointless attempt to escape cuddled up to her majesty downstairs by now," said Morlaak.

Thorr slowly pushed himself to a standing position, and brushed the dirt from his arms and hands.

"You demonstrate a habit of being wrong, Morlaak. I appreciate your consistency, it's helpful, thank you."

Thorr saw that barb hit home.

"You arrogant . . . you're not fit to dig my shit pit," snapped Morlaak. "You don't even have integrity enough for me to want to stain my blade with your blood."

"If you've found another, I'll have that as well," said Thorr.

Ignoring him, Morlaak turn his attention to the sinkhole. "Think I'll let her slowly grind your bones to paste in the pit of her stomach."

Scanning for what to do next, Thorr aimed at stirring Morlaak's ego further to buy time.

"You're a coward Morlaak, an incompetent leader. Every one of your elite has been taken out by an unregistered cadet. When word of your inept leadership and treachery reaches the head of security at Talon West, you'll wish a Bafaalin had consumed *your* bones. That is, if there's enough of you left to stand after our consult."

Morlaak hands dropped from his hips, and his steps became more determined toward Thorr. "I think not. You are to become a sad story. A stain on the honor of your Otaa's name, no matter how you perform next."

"Is that right," said Thorr unaware that something lurking in the shadows crept his way from behind.

"Yes, afraid so, Broz," pressed Morlaak to keep Thorr focused on him. "I'll have to report you died weak and dishonorable. That is after a succession of requests to allow me to take you into custardy to stand trial for your crimes. Unwilling to accept your punishment for the massacre of innocents on the Great North Road. You made your last stand here, a fitting place for one with no future to receive their end."

"You are a disgrace to Scarzen honor Morlaak. No one will believe you," said Thorr, bitter.

"Aww, I think they will. Especially since I have the backing of High Keeper Jallanaa and in front of witnesses, you executed his favorite nephew without quarter in an unsanctioned duel. I've been asked to put miscreant pups like you down before. Now. Are you going to hand over whatever evidence you intended to slander my Keeper's good name?"

Behind, Thorr heard a small sound of shifting gravel but made no attempt to adjust his stance.

"You're going to need to work for it I'm afraid," said Thorr.

Suddenly came the rush of incoming steps. Reacting in complete harmony to meet the oncoming assault, Thorr cast one leg back sliding the long step between his assailant's feet as they brought down a heavy blow. Bent low now facing away from his attacker, Thorr lifted an elbow sharply catching his enemy unawares. Struck center sternum right over their *birth star*, the blow broke the boney shield that protects a scarzen's genitals. Bruxx gasped in agony and buckled at the knees. Groaning with his arms folded holding his chest Bruxx doubled over incapacitated. Thorr raised the same striking arm in a long half circle. Drawing a deep breath at the same time he brought all his weight down hard using the point of his elbow. The falling strike landed on the nape of Bruxx's neck with a heavy crack. Both spines broke killing him outright. It was as if a giant had stomping his bones. Thorr took a short moment to consider the dead warrior at his feet. Then he turned with a scowl toward Morlaak.

"Pups got talent," said Morlaak. "Well done! Didn't expect that outcome. Oh I could have used you to great effect. Pity that sinkhole has to be your end in this life."

Underfoot, Thorr felt the faintest tremor in the earth.

"Do all old wannabe warriors like you talk so much! Stop the nervous words dribbling and drag your sad carcass over here so I can fold your bones and get to dinner, I'm starved," said Thorr.

Morlaak's expression soured to hatred. From scabbards on his belt, Morlaak reached across and drew a kriss with his left hand. The long dagger's ripple shaped blade glinted in the moonlight. With his right, he unsheathed an immaculate, gleaming straight sword. It had an ornate basket weave guard. It was gilded with the coat of arms for the house of the High Keeper of Talon South. He held out the sword pointing the tip toward Thorr.

"Think you have the chest ringers to take down Morlaak, pup? Come closer and learn differently," he beckoned.

"You're still running at the mouth. Do I make you that nervous?" goaded Thorr crisscrossing his impalers as though sharpening razors to carve a roast. "Step up jelly chest. I see the weakness in your knees. Your stalling shows you yearn to be retired."

Morlaak's expression turned to a scowl, and he hurled a kin repel field at Thorr with his dagger filled hand to obscure his charge. Thorr evaded the sizzling teardrop of energy gracefully by leaning back. Tilting one shoulder, he watched it pass by harmlessly. Then, with a bellowing war cry that had true force of its own, Thorr charged in to meet Morlaak.

As both adversaries set to end one another weapons poised, the ground erupted between them throwing them in different directions. The Bafaalin Queen burst upward out of the ground with a banshee's ear piercing squeal. Globules of her larva sprayed in all directions. Her body stretched nearly two stories high, and her hideous orange insectoid face and mouth dripped with the glistening silver strings of her spawn. Both Thorr and Morlaak forgot their exchange momentarily. She remained vertical for a short time before a slow twisting fall to the left. Her head and upper body slammed down right alongside the foundations of the spire with an earth shattering crash. The shockwave shook the ground around so badly, both Thorr and Morlaak attempting to get to their feet were hurled on their backs again. Building foundations around them began to show great cracks, belch stone dust and give way. Thorr saw the spire jolt as if struck by a great hammer. Enormous lightening shaped cracks suddenly sped upward from its underpinnings to the structure's mid-point.

"That's not good," he told himself still on his back.

The top half of the spire began to break into pieces and topple. Tones of dislodged stone blocks fell directly on Thorr's position. Desperately he rolled away like a barrel to avoid being crushed and buried alive. Tons of stone missed him by a mere hand span as the Bafaalin queen continued her thrashing about still spraying silver globules of her larva in all directions. Partly covered in dust and fallout from the collapse, Thorr scrambled to his feet looking for an escape.

Directly in front, he saw Morlaak near the rim of the Bafaalin's sinkhole hurling potent kin barriers at the subterranean terror. One of Morlaak's barriers stuck her in the neck.

"Stop! Thorr bellowed. "You'll end us both Broz!"

Just as Thorr's warning ended, the Bafaalin twisted suddenly in Morlaak's direction and aggressively threw her entire mass to the ground where Morlaak stood.

Thorr saw the ground there give way as though sucked asunder and a larger sinkhole began to open rapidly. The Bafaalin fell through the epicenter of the hole. Morlaak found himself on the fast eroding edge of the sinkhole and slipped away with it. Sounds of a great avalanche taking outpost structures and earth to somewhere far below finally rumbled to a dust cloud disaster-zone of silence. For a moment, Thorr stood there coughing the dust from his lungs. He'd been covered in so much debris he looked like a ghost. He retracted one buckler impaler and wiped his face with the back of his dusty glove.

"Where's that Morlaak? If he's not met his end, he's going to."

Then, at the edge of the hole where Morlaak had fallen, he heard the grumbling curses and gasping of his enemy. He went over to investigate. From a couple of the torches on the walls still aflame, the dull yellow light illuminated the lip of the new sinkhole. Thorr peered over the edge to see a struggling Morlaak clinging to an old tree root exposed from the Bafaalin's final assault. Thorr knelt down placing one arm casually across his knee.

"Deep hole that," said Thorr looking unsympathetically at Morlaak.

Morlaak looked up with a grizzled expression. "You get me out of here Broz or I'll . . ."

"You'll what? Tear my muscular butt a new crack before you find out just how deep her pit goes. Good luck with that."

The root Morlaak clung to jolted as if ready to break.

"I'm going to leave you to the comfort of the hole you intended for me," said Thorr. "Good time to drum up your best words for the ancestors I'd say."

Thorr stood and toed a fist sized rock over the edge of the hole. It toppled and hit Morlaak square on the forehead with a crack. A dribble of blood trickled down the side of Morlaak's face.

"Don't worry, I'll give everyone your best," said Thorr. "No, maybe I should explain your worst. Good for your clan name, don't you think."

Morlaak attempted to pull himself up until the root gave way another notch. He froze and looked down and back up with a sheepish expression.

"Look, I have trilix here on my belt," said Morlaak. "By the look of you, you'll be dead meat in hours if you don't use it. Help me up and I'll give it to you for free, no obligation."

"You keep it," said Thorr. "Where you're going, I think you're going to need it more."

"Grrrr. Broz, I'll have your guts for a necklace if you don't get me out of here. I swear it," cursed Morlaak.

"You just keep working with that," said Thorr turning away heading for the front gate.

"Wait, come back! We can negotiate. Hey! Damn your hide. Listen to me. You need me."

Turning casually away Thorr left the edge of the sink hole. After a few steps he heard more struggle and a final sound of the root Morlaak was holding onto break. He heard Morlaak bark two more profanities before a final yelp as he plummeted into the black.

As he approached the gate, the pain of his injuries began to assert greater intensity now the height of battle had passed. Near the gate's right shoulder amidst fallen debris, dust saturated the light of a lamp that hung crooked on a nearby wall. The illuminated area drew Thorr's eye to a glint of something half buried. Investigating, he uncovered the remains of a broken storage chest and a battered trilix flask. It was still attached to a used utility belt. He looked at it with curiosity.

"Must have been part of the supply being made ready for transport," Thorr said.

Though the container was the worse for wear, it was a quarter full by the weight of it when he pulled it from the belt. It was meant for standard issue by the embossed symbol for the Land Fall Outpost. He removed the lid and applied what remained of the healing liquid to his wounds with the soaked wadding. Immediately there was that familiar tingling burn of healing he'd felt from Trilix many times before. Somewhere behind him, he thought he heard a sigh on the wind, as though someone other than himself also felt relief. It felt good to feel his cracked bones heal in place, and the pain die. He took a minute to gather his thoughts. Somewhere in the darkness behind, though, he heard someone say in a sinister whisper, 'Stronger now, thank you.'

Thorr left Land Fall behind for Talon West and a meeting with the head of security, Dorjaa. He had a tale of conspiracy and murder to tell, one that incriminated a High Keeper at the heart of all of it all. It was news that could shake the whole of Scarza and possibly way beyond.

CHAPTER

12

End of the Line

Thorr arrived at Talon West's southern perimeter on a crisp, clear afternoon. He'd traveled for several days from Land Fall. He was covered in road dust and grime from his forced march and had seen no one on his lonely trail. None save a single sellenor messenger high above winging its way north. That was on the second day. The four-winged messenger sped along as fast as the wind would carry them, not like the gentle riding of the thermals he'd seen them do so often before. Its trajectory pointed direct north, toward the imposing Lyran Mountain Range. Maps and song lines taught the Talon West bunker could be found nestled in the foothills of the range. Thorr had watched the enormous flying mammal until it disappeared into the clouds on the horizon.

After that occurrence, on several occasions during his travels, Thorr felt the weight of someone or something's intelligent eyes on his back. Splinters of concern as to whether Morlaak has somehow scrambled from certain death to pursue him crossed his mind. In every case, he never found the culprit but carried the constant feeling of being stalked. From then on he always walked with one impaler at the ready.

At one point, a recalled song line directed that he trek through a place called The Mossy Valley. The path took him through a dense woodland with a canopy that at times only allowed the thinnest dappled sunlight to penetrate.

This is a bleak and unfriendly place, he thought. *Good for ambush and murder.*

That twisting path saw him emerge heavily assaulted by hordes of insects on Talon West's southern border. Thorr carried a little day dream of happily stabbing the author of *that* particular song line in the face with their pen after his journey through there.

He did remember a day's trek on after that that there was a last easily missed clue in the song line though   *There be more comfortable routes to reach the Talon's Gates. But if one's need is dire, Mossy Valley will deliver feet sooner than later. Beware, the company is not to everyone's taste, for they only seek a willing host.* Trudging along he'd looked skyward to the great and wise ancestor he hoped would hear his pointed thoughts.

"Blood-sucking little snot balls, that's all they were," Thorr grumbled to himself.

Thorr rubbed his cheek where one had left a nasty welt. He knew now he must be close to his objective. He topped the rise of a ridge covered in scrub that had been slashed low recently. Some strides away, in front of that stood a massive corn belt. From his point of view, the field went on for leagues in both direction west and east. It not only provided a source of staple food for the scarzen storehouses inside, but he knew it also served another more sinister purpose. All scarzen settlements used dual purpose defenses like this. The book of War and Strategy labeled this tactic as   Warmth and Sustenance.

His Otaa employed identical tactics in Hammer Forge. This strain of corn grew tall, tall enough to brush Thorr's brow. The scarzen had cultivated the field over many generations. When put to the torch, it burned hot, hot as the sun in mid-season of scorch. With the first white silk due to fall ushering in the next cold season quite soon, the fields looked tinder dry. A gentle breeze from the west giving the field a sway that reminded Thorr of fields back home.

He had to crane his neck to see beyond the field's amber horizon. When he did, he glimpsed a structure on a scale he didn't think possible, even for scarzen masons. Tralldon's descriptions he'd thought in the past to be exaggerated, were, in fact, precise in every detail. Seeing the reality; he now knew his Otaa had been scale correct in every detail. Thorr didn't have a single word big enough in his lexicon to describe to himself what he saw. So he blew a breath between dry lips and whistled a long note to himself in awe of what stood before him. Excited to have a closer look, Thorr found a deliberately cut corridor or Traveler's Funnel as the scarzen called them, for those seeking access to the bunker gates.

This version was just wide enough for two of his race to advance side by side. Once he was walking along the Traveler's Funnel on level ground, he knew, without a doubt, the bunker watch would have eyes on him. He also kept mindful of pit traps on his path, cautious to keep all his limbs intact.

There must be thousands of our warriors to feed inside judging by the size of this field, he thought.

He stepped along the path at as brisk pace. Many strides later, he finally found his way to the other side.

Exiting into the open ground, Thorr saw the well-guarded main gates looming in the mid-distance.

"Naught's beard," he said aloud. "Its length parallels the bunker's entire forward wall in both directions. It's just as Tralldon foretold."

From out here under the orange afternoon sky, the bunker walls resembled a great black tidal wave appearing to stretch for many leagues in both directions. Built from Lyran Mountains black glass-stone, Talon West's walls formed an imposing outer defense stretching nearly eighty feet high. Dome-headed watchtowers stood proud overshadowing the parapet every hundred paces on top of the parapet.

In both directions, the wall ends were lost due to their curvature into the far distance. Thorr surmised they finished somewhere in the foothills of the majestic mountain range behind that supplied the imposing backdrop.

It must have taken many generations to build something such as this, he thought.

He concentrated on the five scarzen warriors of the watch standing at the gate. All of them had eyes on him. An officer, likely the Gate Master in charge stepped forward for a closer look at the possible threat.

Behind the guards, the last vestiges of a drommal caravan being led inside faded into the tunnel's shadows. Thorr took a deep breath.

"Here we go," he told himself and marched straight toward the guards.

***

Those observing Thorr's approach wondered with suspicion as to who the lone young warrior might be, especially heading in from the corn fields so late. All work details had returned a full scan earlier and at a glance, his dress code matched no standard issue inside Talon West the Gate Master was aware of. He did recognize however the possible threat a Maximum Sentinel could be if gone rogue, and this one had clearly seen some action in recent times. They also wore no braid band unit identification or colors to suggest rank.

"Stand fast!" ordered the Gate Master.

Thorr stopped as commanded. From somewhere inside the parapet watchtower overseeing gate activities below, the bunker's night lock-down bells sounded. The change of the watch was standard protocol at this time of day in every scarzen settlement large or small. He now stood just twenty good strides from the gates in full view and knew what the bell warnings meant.

"State your name, clan of origin and business in Talon West."

Thorr presented a respectful bow and customary salute.

"I am Thorr, offspring of Tralldon, Elder of Hammer Forge Outpost. I bring written form of identity and news of a witnessed grave crime.

Respectfully, I ask to speak to Head of Bunker security, Dorjaa. My Otaa is known to him. Security Head Dorjaa is expecting my arrival."

The Gate Master noticeably stiffened at hearing the request. He waved a beckoning hand. "Approach," he ordered.

Thorr walked forward holding a thread of suspicion in the back of his mind wondering if this one could be on Morlaak's payroll. Within arm's length, the Gate Master circled Thorr once with a judging eye.

"If you're dressed for the Day-of-Earth and Ancestors, you're three cycles of the moon too late, warrior," said the Gate Master. His expression pinched, and he leaned in sniffing the air toward Thorr as if something unsavory offended him. "Cor Broz you smell like something a dog threw back up."

"Respectfully Sir," said Thorr. "My journey has not been without incident, and I am here on a matter of urgent business."

The Gate Master shot a sly glance at the subordinates on Thorr's right. "Best be careful of a large Broz such as this one. Why he could positively kill anyone of you with that smell."

Sniggers and scoffs fell from the other warriors' mouths.

"Urgent business you say."

"That's right," said Thorr looking at the Gate Master squarely.

"The only urgent business I can see you have . . . if I let you pass, is where to get an oil bath and less offensive replacement for that repulsive odor engulfing you. You positively reek. What have you been doing, challenging a Bafaalin, ha ha."

More laughs sputtered from the other warrior's mouths enjoying the joke at the stranger's expense. Thorr dropped his gaze squarely upon the Gate Master, who Thorr dwarfed by at least two heads. Thorr's expression turned toward grim as his patience wore thin at being the brunt of a pointless joke.

"Yes, I did," said Thorr. All the chuckling stopped, and the Gate Master's expression turned to surprise when he saw Thorr wasn't joking. "A spawn-dropping Queen actually,' Thorr added. "We disagreed over my intended direction. I explained it to her, once. She refused to give way. I gutted her painfully for the willful blindness to her situation."

All remaining humor died, and scoffs of the other warriors ceased abruptly.

"Now I *really* need to see Head of Security Dorjaa, urgently," said Thorr in a low but determined tone.

The Gate Master cleared his throat and dropped his sarcasm in exchange for the compulsory protocol.

"Why do you bear no sign of unit braid bands or rank?" asked the Gate Master. "What is your unit designation . . . warrior?"

"I have none, Sir," replied Thorr flat.

The Gate Master pulled a surprised expression.

"What! None at all?"

"That is correct, Sir."

The Gate Master's subordinates exchanged glances.

The Gate Master held out one hand. "Identity scroll, or show your brand if you've been outcast."

Thorr reached into his pack as the others looked on. He handed the battered identity scroll cylinder to the Gate Master, who took it with interest. He extracted the parchment within and examined it with a critical eye. A frown of surprise lined the Gate Master's brow. He looked up at Thorr.

"You're just an applicant cadet?" The Gate Master looked up at Thorr in disbelief. "Seriously."

Thorr's apparent connection to officials within the bunker gave the Gate Master cause for pause. Then his public demeanor washed back over his face.

"You outland scrub pups are all the same. Didn't they teach you any protocol out there amongst the rocks? All you had to do was make your position clear."

Thorr tightened his jaw to stop a sharp rebuff.

"A crime you say," said the Gate Master gruffly.

"That's right, Sir. Something Security Chief Dorjaa needs to know, Sir," said Thorr not giving an inch.

The Gate Master rolled the scroll slowly looking at Thorr. He slid it back into the cylinder and slapped it back into Thorr's waiting palm.

"Well, we each have our duty. Whatever you have to say better have some real weight to it, that's all I can say. Old Iron Fist isn't known for his patience, especially with Outland scrubbers."

Behind the Gate Master, a unit of warriors appeared in the mouth of the tunnel for the change of the guard. Swinging a look behind at two of his subordinates, the Gate Master issued some orders.

"You two. Take this trail weathered door-ram directly to Dorjaa. See a bucket of aromatic water is thrown over him *before* he's presented. He stinks worse than a rotting Jaw Fish." He looked at Thorr. "Right, on your way," he ordered thumbing Thorr to move on.

Stepping into the gate entrance, Thorr followed his assigned escort inside Talon West and on to the meeting with the head of bunker security, Dorjaa.

CHAPTER

13

Bad Tidings

At this point of day's end, streets closest to the main gates were busy with citizens making their way to their coming night's activities. Thorr soaked up as much of the bunker's setting as possible. The ordeal of his trek here aside, just being inside the place he had heard of during all of his younger years felt exhilarating. His escorts led him without conversation along several main paved arteries to the west quarter. They passed what appeared to be a market area for dry goods and textiles before stopping at a bath house. There Thorr was permitted some minutes to experience what his escort called Swift Ablutions. The *experience* consisted of him standing against a wall, arms and feet spread as a dump of aromatic water drenched him from overhead. Arms down and a shake of the head with a gasp at the crisp temperature of the water. Then; 'Right he's done', followed by a stiff drying towel hitting him in the face to wipe off the excess, and on their way they went again.

Personal presentation tasks concluded, they walked some distance before passing through two other checkpoints. During that time as they stepped along smartly, somewhere in the mid-distance, he heard several blacksmith's hammers shaping metal. Soon they found themselves outside the front of a rather plain single story structure. It lacked a lot of the finer detail any scarzen building of importance might display. The grounds on the approach boasted modest gardens with a newly erected sign that said; *Textiles Storage*. Outlining the perimeter was a well-tended medium hedge. Unlike other important buildings they had passed, this one had no other official building number. Thorr did, however, see the symbol for *occupied mountain* set into one of large paver along the curving path leading to the entrance. This symbol Tralldon had taught him in the past; usually meant a position of some military significance. Wearers of the symbol were to be respected if encountered, and their orders followed. In scarzen military culture, the upside down V with an arrow up through the center stood for, *Active Security Operations*. Tralldon had told him that those serving with the ASO were a sort of behind the front lines assault force, some of the hardest warriors any bunker put forward in battle. Tralldon stated once that the ASO would be just the sort of job his youngest might be suited for some day, ancestors willing.

Not quite what I was expecting, Thorr thought.

Though, in reality, he didn't really know what to expect.

"On your best behavior, stone breaker," said the leading escort. "You're on Sec Head Dorjaa's turf now."

"Then don't let me hold you back. Lead on," said Thorr.

Built entirely of Lyran Mountain black glass stone, the building's rectangular round-edged structure reached only one single story high. One brazier against the front wall on the left directed the eye to a modest crescent entry; one could easily disregard this destination's importance. One escort lead the way and the three marched off toward the entrance with Thorr in the middle. Closer, Thorr noticed a maximum sentinel standing on guard in the deep shadow opposite the brazier's glow. A warrior clearly of substantial power by his build and armor, they gripped a battle ready polearm with a broad, long curved blackened blade. A weapon an enemy would never see wielded in a night fight. His right shoulder guard displayed the same embossed symbol as the one on the pavement seen behind them.

The guard took one deliberate step forward. "Halt and state your business."

"This individual has just returned from the field," said Thorr's escort. "They have a matter of some urgency to report to Sec Head, Dorjaa. I am directed by Bunker Gate Master to bring in."

Standing at equal height to Thorr, the guard considered him for a moment and then stepped clear granting them entry.

***

Inside, the ASO building's light was low.

This place has a tread careful feel about it, thought Thorr.

By the time they had marched a good twenty strides inside, Thorr had noticed dim lights to several other access points leading who knew where.

Following his escort, something else suddenly dawned on Thorr. His seemingly regular flat-footed guides had much more access to secure places than he would have thought ordinary rank and file should do.

Hmm, perhaps they're not just patrol security after all. Could this be a trap? Might they be part of Morlaak's reach too?

He pushed his paranoia aside but readied himself for any outcome. Their path swiftly led downward via several flights of stairs amounting to three stories below ground by Thorr's calculations. At the end of a short corridor was a single medium sized heavy door, behind which was a sturdy wooden enclosure. Thorr looked over his shoulder questioningly.

"Inside," said the escort.

After a moment of hesitation, Thorr complied. Stepping inside alongside him, they all faced the exit.

"Not keen on little places," said Thorr.

They ignored him. The escort on his left took hold of a handle on the shoulder of the entrance and pulled. Extruding a flexing latticework gate, he locked it off on the other door shoulder sealing them in. Thorr wondered what being inside this breadbox meant. The escort pressed a round wooden panel on the wall next to him. Unexpectedly, Thorr felt a bump from underneath and slowly their enclosure began to sink taking them with it. Thorr saw much stone pass them by in their descent. By the time the transport stopped all he knew was, they were a long way underground.

Exiting the *drop-box*, they made their way along a well lit, polished stone corridor. Of the three doorways in his forward view, they stopped at the second on the right. One of the escorts stepped forward and knocked respectfully on the door.

"Come," ordered a commanding voice.

The escort swung the door inward.

"News from the Outland, Sir," said the escort.

The escort looked back to Thorr and gestured for him to enter. Thorr moved forward as requested.

***

Stepping inside, Thorr heard the door bump shut behind him. He looked back to see he was without the company of his escorts.

The room he stood in was of modest size by scarzen standards. Natural black and gray stone gave the space a sterile feel. To his right, one wall had a thinly padded butt-shelf for any short term visitors. A solid stained Stendle wood desk sat directly in front. Its surface was bare save a carafe containing who knew what with two goblets standing next to it. An ordinary upright chair sat at the front to accommodate a preferred guest. Seated behind the desk, a short, stocky scarzen in well-tailored gray drommal hide armor looked Thorr over with interest. An officer discernible only by his two right braids decorated with three red and gold warrior-of-leadership bands. That meant he was a full commander. Thorr had never met one so high up the command chain before.

His elegant high dark hide collar bore a small gold pin with a red circle and dot in the center. Thorr had no idea what that decoration represented. The office's two left braids ordinarily used to identify the place of birth and commendations had nothing. His demeanor and gaze presented as one in authority. He sat in a high-back chair of Overseer design. Gloved fingers threaded together on top of his desk. An awkward silence passed for a moment or two. Finally, he thumbed his nose thinking on some matter before speaking.

"Well, who might you be then?"

Thorr hesitated. "Ah, Sir. Respectfully, who might I be addressing?"

Hmm cautious, thought the officer. *A good sign, I like that.* "And right you are to ask. Even if said request may take a moment longer to be satisfied."

Thorr frowned. "Sir, before I speak further I must know whom I address."

"Is that so," replied the officer. "I see no braids of rank, no insignia that entitles *you* to request anything."

"Life presents us all with challenges, Sir," said Thorr.

"A warrior's primary function is to achieve victory on and off the field of consultation."

"Hmm. Passage 32 of The Book of Warrior. *Brains and muscle.* Where do you hale from?"

"Respectfully Sir, that was my question to you. Do I or do I not address Chief of Security, Dorjaa?"

The officer nodded. "You do. Now mind how you tread next. Our game is at an end."

Thorr thought for a moment. Instinct told him the chance had to be taken.

"I am Thorr, offspring of Tralldon, citizen of Hammer Forge outpost. Sir, I have but one small final question that will allow me to explain without deception the circumstances under which I come to you today."

"Very well, I like candor, continue."

"If you are Security Head Dorjaa. My Otaa told me you possess a battle memory on your right forearm. It was acquired during the battle of Iron Rock when you fought side by side with him before the massacre."

Dorjaa's face turned grim, and his view fell to his arm on the desktop. "That was a sad time in our history. Ancestors carry him to a better hunting ground."

"My deepest sympathies, Sir. Though your offspring was only two cycles older than I, his courage as a Field Consultant was already widely known."

Dorjaa's darkened mood seemed to lift. "That is heartening to know," he said.

"My Otaa spoke highly of him in his discourse on tactics and warrior potential as inspiration to us. There is now a line sung in his honor passed on amongst our clan. Oraak's loss so soon is a blow to all on the battle front for Talon West *and* Scarza alike."

Dorjaa looked up with a stone hard stare. "One I made the Flaxon pay dearly for many times over in the moons that followed, I assure you."

"Sir, to be sure, with the significance of what I have to tell, may I see the battle memory?"

Dorjaa nodded. "Right you are to ask again."

Looking straight at Thorr the officer loosened the straps securing the forearm guards and right arm sleeve and pulled the sleeve back. On his arm's exposed skin, Thorr saw the beginnings of a lightning shaped scar.

"Good enough?" asked the officer.

Thorr looked carefully at the jagged scar on Dorjaa's arm and then nodded.

"Thank you, Sir. These are my identity papers inclusive of a note from my Otaa, Tralldon, describing events that I'm to bring to your attention."

Thorr handed Dorjaa the cylinder.

"You better have a seat," ordered Dorjaa gesturing to the chair in front of him. "Let me examine this first and then speak of all the details. By the look of this, I'll need everything to make an authentic assessment for actions to come."

"Yes Sir," said Thorr.

Dorjaa extracted and read the information muttering the words unintelligibly. Moments later, he looked up at Thorr apparently thinking hard about what he'd just read.

"Is there more to add?" asked Dorjaa shaking the letter.

"Yes, Sir. A considerable amount, some unpleasant news both shocking and perhaps even inconceivable. But all of it accurate, so I will deliver the accounts without filter."

"Proceed. Leave no splinter to the side."

With that, Thorr began his recollection of last day's events. Listening to the young warrior's story, in general, Dorjaa maintained a face hard to read. But, the moment Morlaak's name and his actions were described, a look of disdain on Dorjaa's face emerged.

Some history there, no doubt, thought Thorr.

Of the duel unlooked for at Hammer Forge and the tragedy of the High Keeper's nephew's death, Dorjaa's only comment was, "That Fits." But the uncovered slave wagons of the Minima women seemed a surprise. When it came to the connection involving High Keeper Jallanaa, Dorjaa seemed almost pleased to hear it. Something in Dorjaa's shift told Thorr the last news eclipsed all the rest. At the report's conclusion regarding the struggle at Land Fall and the murder that took place there, Dorjaa sat back with a grave expression.

"You have brought tools I can work with and confirmed some things that until now were hearsay. You have kept your head in unconventional times and that I like."

"I did the best with the shingles the ancestors tossed, Sir."

Hands clasped on the desk Dorjaa mulled through something then looked directly at Thorr. "How would you like to come and work for me?"

Thorr looked astonished. "Sir I am but a pup, yet to dip his blade in the blood of full field consult. I am not sure what asset I could be."

"I am not the just chief of the ASO here in Talon West, but for all Scarza. The ASO's job is to ensure the inner security, strengths, and vulnerabilities of our most prized assets. We now live in interesting times, and such times call for extraordinary measures."

"What does that have to do with me?" asked Thorr.

What you stumbled into has given us intelligence beyond anything we have had in the past. The agent you unintentionally discovered and rescued had been taken prisoner by Morlaak at the behest of Jallanaa."

"Nattai . . ."

"Yes, Princess Nattai. In the last generation of governance, let's just say progressive thinking amongst some scarzen High Keepers has led to previously unheard of *cooperative alliances.* Immense changes are coming to our lands, recruit. Changes we don't intend getting caught flat footed with."

"Are we going to war?"

Dorjaa looked at Thorr with a blank expression, but there was something behind his gentle gaze, a kind of deeper knowledge or was it wisdom. Being exposed to the short window made Thorr curios.

"Thought we had lost princess Nattai," Dorjaa began. "She went missing with the enemy in the last cycle of the moons. Queen Yazmin of the Minima has been asking questions of late. Things were getting sticky relations-wise between our clans. Then, suddenly, Nattai turned up with another group of Minima woman thought long lost to the slave traders. When she arrived on our safe-house's doorstep near the Minima capital of Gulch, we could hardly believe our luck. The ancestors smiled on us and you that day."

"Wait . . . you know about the High Keeper's slave trade?" asked Thorr.

"Why yes, of course," said Dorjaa with confidence. He leaned forward to pick up the carafe. "Meelow wine? It's our best vintage." Thorr declined with a gentle rise of a palm. Dorjaa filled one vessel for himself. "It has been one of our most lucrative sources of intelligence," Dorjaa said casually.

Thorr sat back, head spinning over the new information.

"The girl had stones, but I never thought of her as *that* kind of warrior. Nor would I have expected such alliances to exist."

"Good, that's how we like it. Nattai told us what took place on the Great North Road, I mean at the wagon train struggle, with that officer of Jallanaa's, Morlaak. She spoke very highly of your courage to save them. With what was hanging over your head already, exposing yourself to a threat of that kind took mettle of remarkable strength."

"Morlaak would have traded those woman like rugs in a bazaar and put down any who opposed him," said Thorr bitterly. "He has," Thorr stalled to correct himself, "make that *had*, no honor worthy of his station. I felt obliged to help him experience the error of his ways."

"You represent the honor of your clan well scarzen. By speaking of Morlaak in past tense, I take it you saw he was well chastised?"

"On my last sighting of him, Morlaak and a Bafaalin Queen were discussing terms at the bottom of her sinkhole."

"Excellent news," said Dorjaa. "Couldn't happen to a nicer Broz."

"He was after this," said Thorr passing Dorjaa the trilix flask he was carrying. "One of the slave trading Wagon Masters had it on him. If it wasn't stolen, which didn't seem likely to me the way he concealed it. It had to be payment for service rendered. A service of an expensive nature judging by the zeal my pursuers had for wanting to stop me reaching you here."

Dorjaa took the flask and inspected it with a critical eye.

"This is part of High Keeper Jallanaa's personal stock. Treasured by the soft skins outside our borders. Good, I'll send a unit to investigate both Land Fall and the Wagon incident further, just to be sure."

"Now, what happens?" asked Thorr.

"Well, the thing is . . . what to do with you now? I think calls for your conviction will present you with both freedoms and problems of equal strength with recent events."

"How so," asked Thorr.

"Well, with the hopeful loss of Morlaak and his unit there is no eyewitness for the prosecution. That doesn't mean shadows of the night will not always be shadows. There will be those who will seek your end if the opportunity presents. Morlaak stood as Jallanaa's behind the scenes enforcer, a position of privilege he enjoyed. You have upset the scales of intrigue in scarza removing him as you've done. Jallanaa will not be pleased to know of his loss." Dorjaa leaned forward. "But there are those, like me, who applaud your show of fortitude and integrity in the face of such odds."

Thorr sat there one eyebrow raised. He had the feeling the gate of one life's path just silently closed behind him, while another path, until now unknown, stood directly in front. Dorjaa grunted and nodded, *decision made*, his mind made up about something.

"So how about that job then?"

"What kind of a job are we talking about?" Thorr asked frowning.

"One of an ah, unorthodox nature. I think you might be just the instrument I need to help in something that is likely to change the entire face of Scarza. I'd like to employ you as one of ASO's sleeper agents.

"What does that mean. Who do I have to consult with," asked Thorr his curiosity peaked.

"The breaking of bones will be an aspect of your duty as circumstance provide. But more importantly, it's your eyes, ears, and resourcefulness that will be your main staple for the time being. If you accept; you will be under my protection, which has considerable weight and influence. But it also means you will find yourself placed in harm's way when called upon."

"Won't I stand out? I mean, I'm not exactly easy to hide, and my kin ability isn't anywhere near a Stealth Engineer's strength."

Dorjaa smiled. "You have the enemy at a disadvantage already. It's your hidden intellect and strength that interests me. They *expect* to see a wall breaker like you in plain sight. Many of my best agents are hidden just that way. All you need do is play to their belief of you being a little umm green on the uptake."

"And, what if word *has* reached High Keeper Jallanaa about what happened? Will he not want a head? I cannot guarantee *all* were eliminated. I only consulted with five of them. Morlaak could have had a seven tear unit."

"Let me worry about that. You are quite safe within the walls of Talon West. We'll send out some disinformation placing you in Talon North. High Keeper

Keenass and Jallanaa have a less than cordial relationship. Jallanaa's spies are very thin on the ground in the North.

"Your reach in Scarza seems considerable," said Thorr.

"I make do," said Dorjaa. "Until contacted, you would merely go about your ordinary obligations. Your induction will go ahead as planned, tomorrow. You are just another hopeful looking to bring honor to Scarza."

"We'll arrange something more flavorsome to keep any interest Jallanaa may have in you shall we say, distracted. If all you have told me is true, High Keeper Jallanaa will do nothing in the open about Morlaak's activities. No doubt, though, when he realizes his loss and potential exposure, he will be most displeased. He will likely offer a stooge to take his fall as he has always done in the past."

"I see," said Thorr with a tone of concern.

"While you are here, your new allies will have eyes on you. In a pinch, be as resourceful as you have shown you can be. From what I now understand you will be very hard to put down."

"My Otaa Tralldon always seemed to think so."

"If memory serves well, Tralldon carries some of those traits himself. I have witnessed many try to best him in open consult. The ancestors were always there to welcome them after Tralldon efficiently sent their spirit on."

Thorr sat there, thinking deeply on what had passed and what was on off.

"So . . ." said Dorjaa. "Are we agreed? Do you accept my offer?"

"Yes, Commander," said Thorr. "I am honored to be at your service."

Dorjaa shuffled in his seat with satisfaction.

"Good! Your code name shall be. . ." Dorjaa thought for a moment, "Mace. Only myself, Staask on the other side of that door behind you and High Keeper

Malforce of Talon East will know that. Staask will be your *Whisper.* Should anything need to be passed your way, you'll receive it from him or me personally. At induction tomorrow, you will be paired with someone we have an interest in. A Talon East inductee named, Beetaa Pinnaraa."

"What has he done?"

"Your task, agent, is simply to keep eyes on, not to pass judgment. Keep anything Beetaa Pinnaraa does out of the ordinary ready to hand over if contacted. Can you be that adaptable thinking field agent I'm looking for? You will be put in harm's way to protect the interests of Scarza; you understand that?"

"Sir being put in harm's way is what all scarzen are bred for. If it keeps me out of the slaa groves and helps restore my Otaa's good name, then you have my blade hand on it."

Dorjaa smiled. "Good. Your first assignment will be to gather information. Observe Pinnaraa's actions, there are some important plans for him in Talon East, and we want to be sure we have the right individual."

"You shall know of the dust that puffs from under his boot souls if it stands out."

"Good. High Keeper Jallanaa threatens the very status quo of Scarza's hierarchy. We have been trying to uncover his real operation for the past ten moon cycles. He is a shrewd one and ruthless as are his agents. He is aiming to have all of Scarza under his heel." Dorjaa looked toward the door. "Staask."

The door swung inward and one of the guards that had escorted Thorr into the building entered.

"Staask, see agent Thorr here is processed for induction into the academy's Blue Squad under Sergeant Zaxaa without interruption."

"Yes, Sir."

"Let the Eye know we have another *ant on the ground*." Dorjaa gestured for Thorr to stand and follow Staask. "Oh and Staask."

"Sir."

"See he gets a real bath this time and an alternative to what he's wearing. He should present as un-trail weary as possible. Right now a Snaak wouldn't piss on him, he positively reeks."

"Yes, Sir."

Thorr saluted Dorjaa, turned and moved to the door following Staask out into the corridor. The door closed with a bump that marks the end of one life and the beginning of another and some unexpected turns to come.

CHAPTER

14

A New Dawn

Next morning;

At the Talon West Academy's sunbaked dusty induction parade ground, eighty-nine sponsored cadets including Thorr gathered for registration. Some apparently knew one another, others like Thorr stood out as individuals. He wondered who Beetaa Pinnaraa might be amongst them. His escorts from the night before had provided an acceptable change of armor. It had different patterning and build signature from an armorer in Talon East to better help with his cover. The garb was an older design but well-made. Much better than the rough outpost initiate's version he'd cast aside. They'd offered a choice of basic weapons to finish his façade too. He accepted the armor but kept his bucklers. He wasn't parting company with them; they were handed down to him from three generations.

Recruits for this induction were from all over Scarza, bunkers and outposts alike. The braids on many inductees showed a high dominance from Talons East and North, with locals from Talon West rounding out the rest. Thorr was the only representative from Scarza's southern regions. Nobody knew him at all.

Thorr hadn't slept much the night before. His mind stirred endlessly wondering about his interview with Dorjaa and how all the pieces fitted together. Glancing about the gathering before the on-parade call sounded, he wondered who was *the Eye* Dorjaa spoke of. How many spies aside from himself might be in this collection of hopefuls? His mind nattered with all that had passed in last days. Thoughts of Morlaak's actions, their consult at Land Fall and the clan members Thorr had been forced to dispose of, still held sway in his mind. What might the future hold for him now? A loud, deep tone from the academy's Twist-shell Horn sounded arresting the muttering and banter of voices. Another blast to assemble from the Twist Shell Horn sounded. All cadets looked to nearby officers for commands to be given. In front of them, a red sandstone podium made specifically for inductions like this stood prominently at the front of the parade ground. A heavy-set drill sergeant wearing a red lanyard and ceremonial sash stepped into plain view next to the podium.

"Cadets form up!" he boomed. "Feet on the marked lines boneheads. Step lively now!"

Thorr saw the many yellow lines marked using chalk dust and moved to comply with the others. All focused their attention on forming ranks in front of Talon West's Estan military instructors who had stepped forward to direct traffic.

In moments a column formed up at attention. A broad-shouldered officer with thick dreadlocks and many battle commendation bands on his braids stepped on to the podium.

"I am Koraa, Master Law Enforcer in Talon West. Bring here only that which will serve Scarza well and do your clan name honor. However you have behaved in the domains of your birth is of no consequence to me. How you behave here is. You will have heard many names given to this Academy, not used by Talon West's architects. Kuzaa, Zornaaz Dumaak, but you need to remember only one, the correct one, Taozen. For it is within these walls you will be molded into the stuff of legend. You are here you have your potential revealed in every area of endeavor a scarzen is bred for. It is here, *you*, become Scarza's Taozen; *the storm that breaks the enemy.*

Koraa emphasized the last sentence with a raised fist. "Like those before you, you shall become the storm that breaks the will of all who contest Scarza's strength. It can be you our allies look to for victory in the midst of the worst consult."

Standing with the others, hearing Koraa speak, Thorr soaked up the atmosphere with a welcome heart. He filled with pride in what it meant to be scarzen. For a moment, being a front-line shock warrior was all he wanted his life to be. During the last year in preparations for his rite-of-passage, he'd met some strong warrior mentors who had told stories of Taozen. But these officers standing before him now seemed far larger in real life than the song lines tossed about back at Hammer Forge around the camp fires. But being here, Thorr felt something very different. Powerful figures such as Law Enforcer Koraa would give pause to the toughest rebel cadet who might want to step out of line.

"Before I have the pleasure of introducing your Commandant," boomed Koraa. "I say this to you all. Regardless of clan status or perceived *special* dispensations you think you possess, in Taozen none are above the law. Here all are equal under Academy administration. There is no Otaa to speak on your behalf here or Otutt to ease your bruised pride when we expose your flaws. In short, time to suck it up pups. In the event you are to be disciplined, your greatest hope should be that you *not be* sent my way. Here all transgressions are dealt without favor for clan ties. Bear that in mind cadets next time any of you consider making a mark that will draw my attention."

To Thorr's left, the cadet beside him muttered; "He's tough."

Thorr glanced down for a moment at the wiry framed individual who'd spoken. Their eyes remained straight ahead. Their braid bands told Thorr they were from Talon East. The warrior's build suggested he was bred for the engineering cast. He fitted well the frame of a stealth insurgency warrior, one of the subcategories of an engineer. Unlike Thorr's cast intended for breaking front lines and stronghold walls, this one would be light and very fast on his feet, bred to be a devil to deal with in close quarter consult. Koraa's voice drew Thorr's attention back.

"Follow orders! Make Scarza proud!" Koraa relaxed his posture. He placed a dark gloved hand at the top of the pedestal in front of him supporting a thick black bound tomb.

"May each of you swiftly live up to the potential your letters of introduction indicate. Proudly, I now hand you over to Academy Commandant, Zaastaa."

Thorr watched Koraa step to one side. Presenting a short bow and right cheek forward, Koraa then gestured for Commandant Zaastaa to address the column. Zaastaa acknowledged Koraa with a polite tilt of her head and stepped to the podium to speak. She stood short in stature compared to those around her. Her slight build, darker complexion, and long weighted ponytail slung over her right breast common to the western clans, contradicted the audacity and fierceness in a consult she was known for. Across the land, her reputation was legendary.

Standing with the other inductees, Thorr could feel the strength exuded by Zaastaa as her gaze swept past him from one cadet line to another. Finally, Zaastaa spoke with a clear commanding delivery: "Cadets, stand ready!"

The ranks snapped to attention. A clap of boots echoed across the parade ground. Zaastaa looked forward and to her right where a heavy-set officer stood nearby. Dressed in fitted slaa-thread black battle dress and gauntlets, he had several commendation bands on his braids. He also wore the Lanyard of Courage, one of the highest honors a scarzen could achieve on the battlefield. She acknowledged him with a small nod before speaking.

"Cadets, welcome to the rest of your life! All are here to take a standard and order-of-the-march. I oversee every induction at Taozen Academy. I am your Taozen Otutt for the time of your stay. Excel and there are many rewards. Shy away from your duty and you will find Taozen less than accommodating. You are the chosen elite each clan has to offer. But remember this. Perfection here is not an ideal   it is a requirement. As Master Law Enforcer Koraa has stated, there is only one law here! Taozen Law. Do not test my or my staff's resolve by pressing that boundary. Taozen's Attitude Correctional Arm's ability to have transgressors see the error of their ways is, I assure you, most effective!"

"There goes the neighborhood," said the warrior to Thorr's left that had caught his attention before.

"You will know only those within Taozen walls for the duration of your stay," Zaastaa continued. "No outside communication is permitted, without *my* express authority. Expect to be pushed to your limits during your assessments. It is after all why you are here. Knowing the truth of your skill-sets potential to us is paramount. Passing your first threat assessment will see you placed for specialization. Succeed there; you will be free to choose a battle ally from amongst your squad. A flawed choice of battle ally could cost Scarza victory, and you your life. So when the time comes, think carefully on that. Those decisions made, you will then both go on to full service in a lifelong bond. Only supreme warriors gain the privilege of wearing our coveted Taozen tattoo of the starburst and sickle on their neck. Those who do not reach expectations *will* be sent to standard troop detachments or agricultural support posthaste."

Zaastaa looked to an officer directly in front. "Taozen Roll Master, assign them," she ordered.

The Academy Roll Master faced her and saluted. Then with a crisp snap of heels, he about-faced. Using a sharp, commanding tone gave the next order.

"Cadets! When called, raise your right fist. Identify yourself and your clan," he ordered. "Each Rank Drillmaster will take charge of their squad as the role is defined."

Answers to the roll rang out as the commandant oversaw proceedings. She stood with her back straight. Resting her hands upon the address stand, Thorr watched her glance at the pages of the now open tomb. Each called name was responded to by an enthusiastic cadet.

***

Finally, the ranks stood by silently as a stiff breeze blew swirling red dust through their ranks and across the parade ground. Thorr felt the warrior on his left who had spoken earlier had a strange aura about them.

What might you be?

The warrior's attention seemed to stir as if they'd heard Thorr's musing. Zaastaa's voice pulled his attention back.

"Your integrity as warriors of Scarza is inspiration for clans who follow. Your Drillmaster's word is final in all matters connected with you."

Another gust of wind and dust whistled through the ranks. Thorr thought he heard a whisper accompany that second wind as it passed by. *Take heed.* Then he heard another voice inside his head, unthreatening.

She's tough!

The feeling for the comment's origin came from the warrior next to him again. Thorr provided a guttural grunt of acknowledgment and felt the warrior's attention swing his way. They glanced at Thorr.

"Pinnaraa, Talon East," they said softly.

Internally, realizing he had found his target so early somehow unsettled Thorr.

"Thorr, Talon South," he replied from the corner of his mouth.

They both noticed the Drill Master to their right turn and walk their way slowly.

"Heard that. You're sentinel caste?"

"However did you work that out? Was it the size of my boots?"

"Tall tree like you should be with the other rock breakers."

"Caste transgressions have consequences."

They paused their whispering as the drillmaster drew closer. Stopping for a moment, he placed his focus on a cadet only strides away. Pinnaraa glanced up and noticed the rite-of-life birthmark in the shape of a lightning bolt exposed on Thorr's neck. Pinnaraa's view then dropped to the vacant trilix flask slot on Thorr's battle belt. His sentinel belt band was missing too replaced with one for standard field force service. Pinnaraa frowned. The commandant addressed the rank and file again.

"A small number of you may even be drafted into the Myst corps," Zaastaa said.

"That's me," Thorr and Pinnaraa both whispered in tandem.

"I now hand final selection procedure over to Commander Koraa. Good luck Cadets."

Koraa stepped forward.

"Column pay respect. Atten . . . tion!" The entire column braced, arms snapping straight down by their sides. "Stand at . . . ease!" Each Warrior spaced feet one shoulder width apart as if shunted by a heavy spring. "Last night, your braids will have had an addition added for academy identity: first, the color identifies your new squad to which you will be assigned. Second, it is used in the event of your death to identify you. IS THAT CLEAR?" Zaastaa boomed.

"HO!" the rank and file roared in response.

Spaced well enough to oversee a quarter of the column each, stood a Drillmaster—an NCO who would be their training instructor and overall watchdog. Each Drillmaster wore the yellow and red oval insignia of a battle hardened field unit commander on their right breast. A few short paces away from each Drillmaster stood a unit commander or Roll Master. The first of those stepped forward and bellowed an order.

"RED SQUAD! FORM UP BEFORE ME!" ordered their Roll Master.

His booming command met the furthest edges of the parade ground. Immediately, thirty cadets from amidst ranks wearing red braid bands advanced to form up in front of the rest in two straight lines. He looked them over with an experienced eye and turned to his subordinate.

"Drillmaster, take them to barracks," came the Roll Master's second command.

"Yes Sir," replied the Drillmaster taking one step forward. He paused to salute his superior and then faced his squad.

"Red Squad, Drillmaster Shaa calls you to order!"

"HO!" came the column's united reply.

"As one, by my command," Shaa ordered, "Le-eft face!"

Already well-disciplined from pups war school, all the Red Squad cadets turned ninety degrees left in two short clean steps. The sound of their boots clapped the ground producing a faint echo.

"By the left," ordered Shaa. "Forward march!"

Combined the column surged forward leaving the parade ground accompanied by their new Drillmaster and commanding officer. The next commanding Roll Master called his column to order.

"Green Squad, FORM UP BEFORE ME!"

Just like the one before those with green braid bands stepped forward. One straggler who popped into plain view looking lost appeared to have been pushed by another. He stood there for a moment looking back over his shoulder awkwardly.

The Green Squad Drillmaster stepped forward. He stood out as a hard faced individual with a high forehead and pointy chin. He issued commands in a shrill voice;

"Have you lost your apron string Pup?" Barked the Drillmaster. "You're with that lot," he said sarcastically, pointing. As the cadet shuffled into position the Drillmaster tossed a rolled eye look to to his Commander. "My first short list reject, Sir." The Drillmaster looked back to the cadet. "Don't fail me on such short notice pup! We haven't even seen you sweat yet."

A few subdued chuckles filtered forward from the remaining ranks.

"Drillmaster, assume command," ordered the Roll Master.

"Yes, Sir," relied the Drillmaster. "Drillmaster Shinexx calls Green Squad to order! LEFT FACE. March ON!"

"HO!" came a strong reply from the column, voices in slight disarray. *Stomp, stomp, stomp*, their heavy boots pounded the earth as they filed off the parade ground, command staff urging them on.

"Our turn," Thorr muttered to himself. He glanced to Pinnaraa beside hime. *Let the games begin.*

The last Roll Master, an officer with the front half of his head shaved called the last orders.

"Blue Squad Drillmaster, assume your command."

The Drillmaster concerned stepped forward to claim his responsibility. His voice had a rasp sound to it, as if he'd been bellowing orders too much all his life.

"Drillmaster Zaxaa calls Blue Squad to order!"

Thorr thought he sounded like an excited gravel crusher.

All bearing blue braid bands formed up. Pinnaraa took their place again close to Thorr.

"Blue Squad, by my command," ordered Zaxaa. "Riiiight face! By the left, March ON!"

The strength of Zaxaa's final command jolted Blue Squad to reply in a unified, "HO!"

The rank tilted forward as one and boots in time they marched off. As Thorr marched with the rest, he watched Beetaa Pinnaraa in step directly in front.

So, what have you done or are going to do? he wondered. *What interest can Dorjaa have in you?*

Thorr's active mind quickly shifted into high curiosity. The rank left the parade ground with high hopes for the dawn of their future glory as scarzen warriors. As they left the parade ground, Thorr thought he glimpsed a man like figure observing them from the shadows. At his right boot sat a dog.

CHAPTER

15

Epilogue

On a small plateau on the shoulder of Mount Lyran behind Talon West, a small concealed camp overlooked activity below. Uniss stood contemplating recent unfolding events. His companion, a stocky Blue Heeler sat next to his right boot looking at the same activities with intelligent eyes.

"Hmm, things are stickier than I thought, Dogg."

"Yes. H is up to something Uniss, I can feel it in my fur. And those two scarzen are right in the thick of it. Now the Agent is here, best wrap it up, we have a lot to sort out."

"I reckon you're right Dogg. Okay Agent, before we jump time to see where this takes us, best you know a couple of things. For Thorr, life is about to get *very* interesting. There is a lot coming his way. A future role he never could have imagined now stands before him. Thorr, along with a human called Ben Blochentackle, our apprentice as it happens, is a grand part of all to come. It's a journey Thorr can't even begin to fathom, and since you're along for the ride, nor will you at first. In our experience life isn't meant to be . . . predictable.

We have evidence that Thorr and his new associate, Beetaa Pinnaraa, have been part of a sinister plot from the moment they were born from the chest. This is no ordinary planet, Agent. What you don't know is this. Tora is a prison world. A world specifically created by the Evercycle Council to incarcerate one infamous individual, Herrex Lord of Balance. We believe the two scarzen in our investigation are a part of Herrex's grand plan to be made whole once more. There isn't a prison in the Superverse that can hold him except Tora, and something unworldly is very wrong with Tora's workings right now. So, where you're concerned Agent, we will meet again too, soon. You might not at first remember us, but when you do, remember this too, nothing's as it seems.

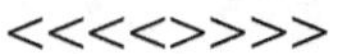

About the Author

Yuan Jur served in the Australian military as a young adult. He later sought the solitude of monastic life serving the community as an ordained Buddhist monk for many years. In Buddhism's warrior-caste arm known in the West as Zen he achieved the rank of abbot and theologian. As a theologian, Yuan Jur studied many belief systems, doctrines and ideologies from around the world. During those decades he also gained a master's degree in Chinese martial arts and medieval weaponry.

In 2007 a life threatening illness ended his monastic career and nearly his life. During recovery, Yuan Jur turned to a new venture. He combined his knowledge gained from decades of belief systems study with a love of Time Travel Paranormal alt/world fantasy as a young man. The result was a totally new immersive superverse series called Citadel 7. By 2014 his first Citadel 7 series combined trilogy had won both blue ribbon and Grand Prize in the Chanticleer Cygnus international writing Awards. He states: "There is a lot, lot more to come."